About the Author

Craig Smith lives in Musselburgh with his wife, two children, a cat, and Scotland's oldest goldfish.

He's been many things in his time, but by far the most challenging was washing dishes in a Mexican restaurant (all that baked-on cheese is a nightmare to clean). Nowadays, when not scraping a living building web sites, he occasionally dusts off his bass guitar and joins one of his old bands on the nostalgia circuit. This led to him waking up hungover and naked with his bandmates in a Tokyo bathhouse at 7am, so it's not all pipes and slippers (although it was very hard getting out of that bath). He's the proud recipient of two NME singles of the week and four Ks in Kerrang, which he's tempted to get tattooed on his arm but is worried he'd chicken out after three.

The Mile is his debut novel, and was written feverishly, fuelled by the pressing nature of the independence debate. His next book will be longer.

D0255915

The Mile

Craig Smith

Pilrig Press

YA

Published 2013 by Pilrig Press, Edinburgh, Scotland

Copyright © Craig Smith 2013

The right of Craig Smith to be identified as the author
of this work has been asserted by him in accordance with the
Copyright Designs and Patent Act 1988.

All rights reserved.

A CIP catalogue record for this book is available on request
from the British Library.

This novel is entirely a work of fiction. The names, characters and incidents
portrayed in it are the work of the author's imagination. Any resemblance
to actual persons, living or dead, events or localities is entirely coincidental.

ISBN 978-0-9566144-8-3

www.pilrigpress.co.uk

Printed by Martins The Printers
Berwick-upon-Tweed

Pilrig Press

For Sophie & Riley

Pilrig Press is an independent micro publisher based in Edinburgh. We're passionate about books but do not have budgets for marketing them. If you enjoy The Mile, we would be chuffed to bits if you would tell your friends, write a review, or spread the news on your social network of choice.

Thank you.

Acknowledgements

Thanks are due to Marc at Pilrig Press for taking a chance on an unknown writer, and to Anne Hamilton for the words of encouragement.

Big thanks to my wife Fiona, for putting up with me when all this was written. And to Sophie and Riley for remembering who I was when I emerged from the loft.

Finally, thanks to anyone involved in the #indyref discussion on Twitter. Many of our conversations have played a part in the creation of this book.

CHAPTER ONE

The Esplanade, Edinburgh Castle

The slate roofs and weathered copper domes of Edinburgh's New Town stretched out before him. The late afternoon sun dancing over the sandstone, shone down between light autumn clouds blowing over from the west.

Ian took in the view from the castle esplanade; the regularity of the Georgian streets, bordered above by the cold grey ribbon of the Forth and below, by the bustle of Princes Street. He wondered how different the view might have been if the original plan for the New Town had gone ahead, with diagonal streets cutting from each corner, mirroring the flag of the union. Instead, the bastards had to settle for making Thistle Street shorter than Rose Street, a subtle reminder to the residents of Northern Britain that England would forever regard herself as their superior.

He watched the buses trundle along the architectural mish-mash of Princes Street. It had its critics, but Ian didn't mind the occasional concrete eyesore, muscling in between the intricate facades of older buildings like badly-fitted dentures. It showed Scotland was a forward-looking nation - willing to change, and ready to re-invent itself. And if ever there was a time for that it was now. The street, like the country, was in decline. The great shops of the past were slowly being replaced by junk shops selling Chinese-made tartan crap to Japanese tourists, and generic discount clothing emporiums selling cheap clothes to a Scottish population that was fast losing its identity. While other shops, more tellingly, sold nothing; their windows covered by plywood, or metal shutters, gathering posters and spray paint.

On the plus side, it made for an easy life at work. At the Registers of Scotland there was nothing worse than a healthy economy. At times like that, title deeds and boundaries were altered frequently as buildings changed hands, or merged, or were demolished and rebuilt. With the country stagnating after years of recession, there wasn't a lot of movement, so the paperwork was kept to a minimum. As a result, they'd banned overtime, and this was the last thing he needed right now. But with time on his hands he had managed to take the work's first aid course - something that, since having kids, he'd been keen to do. And he'd now been put on archiving duties, sorting through boxes of paperwork and scanning ancient title deeds and maps in a race to digitise everything. And where would that lead? Probably job losses eventually, but for now, it would have to do. Okay, it wasn't brain surgery, but it was a job - one that he'd been doing for fifteen years, and had the promise of a fairly decent pension at the end of it. Or at least it did, until Westminster decided it was the public sector that had caused the financial meltdown and raided their pensions to bail out the banks.

He scanned the street below. The Friday-night rush of workers created a blur of activity along the shop-fronts. On what used to be his favourite record shop, he could make out a huge display of "UK-OK" posters - promoting the unionist campaign in next week's independence referendum. OK? He shook his head, is that the best they can offer? He looked further along the street and smiled when he finally spotted a larger cluster of "YES" banners. Not long now, he thought.

He'd been on a mission lately - arguing in pubs, and at work, with anyone who'd trotted out the usual reasons for maintaining the status quo: We're better together; we couldn't manage on our own; we'd lose our standing in Europe; we can't afford it. They didn't get it. Things had to change. Every word uttered by the unionists was based on fear and what-ifs. Negativity vs positivity. Bitterness vs hope. Despite his glum demeanour, Ian was, at heart, at optimist and he couldn't understand the lack of vision he saw in his fellow countrymen. If every supporter of independence converted just one pro-union voter, the job would be done - more than that, it'd be a landslide. Had he managed this? He was pretty sure, and he was going to give it his best shot tonight too.

He checked his watch - five o'clock. He was on time, as usual. He stuck his hands in the pockets of his old corduroy jacket and turned his back on the view, leaning against the railings just in time to see a thin figure in a black leather jacket attempt to dodge his way towards him through the throng of tourists. A woman in a luminous hiking jacket charged towards the castle gates, going against the flow. She knocked into the man in black, uttered a hurried apology and kept running for the entrance - last entry was at 5pm; she'd be lucky, he thought. Ian laughed as his friend Euan stood shaking his head at the woman and straightening his jacket. What had they called him at University? Calamity. The unluckiest man in Scotland. Ian chuckled to himself and stepped forward to meet him.

"Euan my man, still got a way with the ladies I see?"

"Ian! What the hell is that on your chin?"

Ian grabbed the hand of his old friend and shook it. Then with a shrug, laughed and pulled him close for a hug.

"Nice to see you too, as usual," he said, slapping his back. "This, my man, is a beard, they're all the rage I believe. You should get one."

"Aye okay, run that past my wife will you?" said Euan, disengaging from the hug and stepping back to look up at Ian's new facial growth. It grew in a wild tangle, mirrored by the ginger mess on top of his head. "You look well. Apart from having enough hair for both of us." Euan ran his hand over his bald head, "I think my last few stragglers have abandoned ship, so to speak. So, how's things? Give me five years in a nutshell."

"In a nutbag, Euan, things are good," said Ian, smiling. "Still living the dream at the Registers. Two kids, as you know. One of each. Both wee bastards. You know all this anyway, fucking Facebook. What are folk meant to talk about these days when they actually meet up?"

Euan laughed. "Aye I know, I've been following your developments. But you'll know this with all the 'likes' I've been hitting you with. So, now that we're all caught up..." he shrugged, "I'll see you in another five years aye?" He turned, as if to leave.

"Aye, okay, nice, see you later..." joked Ian. "No, there is one other thing that I haven't made public yet. Shona's pregnant again."

Euan beamed. "Congratulations!" He grabbed Ian by the hand again and shook it vigorously. "Jesus, she's a glutton for punishment your Shona. Never understood what she saw in you to be honest. Any idea what you're getting?"

"Nope," smiled Ian, "just got the 12 week scan. All's well, but we don't really want to know, as long as they're healthy and all that eh?"

"It'll be ginger though."

"Oh aye," Ian frowned, "It'll definitely be ginger!"

Euan laughed, and thought of Ian's wife Shona. He hadn't seen her in years but god she was gorgeous. Flame-haired and funny. They had it all. Lucky bastards. Okay, they were rammed into a two-bedroom flat just off Leith Walk but he envied their closeness. He thought of Vicki, probably halfway through her first bottle of wine by now, staring at the TV in their roomy and well-appointed Georgian flat on Royal Terrace, looking out over the treetops of London Road gardens. The flat had three bedrooms, none of them painted bright pink or blue. All a faded magnolia. And recently, only one of the bedrooms hadn't been in use. Euan had taken to sleeping in the smallest room, at the back of the flat. As far from Vicki as the confines of their home together would allow.

Ian continued, "So what about you? You're the fucking invisible man on Facebook. Other than the occasional 'thumbs up' you've not exactly shared much. I'm hoping you've got plenty tales to tell?"

"Oh, plenty time for that Ian. We've got the whole night ahead of us. No wives. Just three mates, a wallet full of money and a shitload of boozers. Why the Royal Mile by the way? Sick of Broughton Street?"

"Don't know," said Ian, not entirely truthfully, "just fancied a wee change, that's all."

Euan rubbed his hands together, "Well, wherever we end up, I'm not fussed, just glad to be out. Where the hell's Stuart anyway?"

Stuart hurried up the steep slope of Market Street, the sprawl of Princes Street gardens to his right. He was glad to be out of that train. Four and a half hours stuck opposite an overweight, over-friendly and overly made-up English woman who stank of salt and vinegar crisps and grimaced each time her nose fizzed with diet coke burps. She'd engaged him in an unwanted conversation as they'd left King's Cross and refused to take the hint, even when he'd started untangling his iPod headphones.

By Darlington he'd managed to put one earphone in, and was thumbing through tracks while occasionally nodding, or shaking his head, or sighing and tutting at her seemingly endless tales of woe. She was off to Edinburgh to meet her sister, for a weekend of shopping and eating to ease the pain of her recent disastrous relationship. He'd walked out on her, left her for a girl at his office, skinny little bitch. Stuart was losing the will to live.

She'd finished the diet coke, bought six mini bottles of white wine from the buffet trolley and her chat seemed relentless. Eventually though, perhaps sensing his increasing irritation, she offered, "So, sorry love, enough about me."

You're not wrong there, thought Stuart.

"What about you? What do you do? What have you got waiting for you in Edinburgh?" She poured herself another wine.

Stuart sighed, removed the earphone and clicked his iPod off. "Erm, just a night out with some old friends. We meet up every few years, catch up, lie about how well we're doing, you know?"

"Right...." she waited for more, but it wasn't forthcoming. "And how well are you doing?" To be fair to her, she was doing all the work.

Stuart looked out of the window at the passing fields. "Alright I guess. Don't spend a lot of time here to be honest." Reluctantly, he continued, "I'm a travel writer, well hotel reviewer, that sort of stuff. And I've got a wee place in France I'm doing up. Suits me fine. As long as I've got my laptop and an internet connection. That's all I need."

The train powered northwards and he went on, describing the house in France. Yes, it needed a lot of work. No, it wasn't very big. Yes, the weather was much better. No, he didn't get to Paris much. The house was too far south, - in the Limousin, where property was cheaper.

She downed her last wine, and was looking at his lips while he talked. "So, no girlfriend?" She ran one finger around the rim of her plastic tumbler.

"Nope. Look I'm pretty knackered sorry, I've come straight

off the Eurostar and onto this train. And I need to, erm, I've got this thing, on here, I need to listen to," he said, pointing at his iPod and untangling the headphones. He smiled at her, plugged himself in and stared out the window. He watched her reflection. A knowing smile on her lips, she raised her eyebrows, gave an exaggerated sigh and pulled a paperback book out of her bag. Something about a child locked in a cupboard, by the look of the cover.

An hour of Mazzy Star on the iPod, and he was fast asleep. He was woken by the bustle of travellers around him and the screech of the train's brakes as they approached Edinburgh's Waverley Station.

"At least you got a kip," she said, "you'll be fresh for your night out. Nice meeting you..." she belched quietly as she struggled out of her seat, dusted crisp crumbs off her sizeable chest and wobbled slightly as she side-stepped into the aisle. "My name's Sharon, by the way. Maybe see you again?" You had to give her full marks for trying.

"Erm, yeah, I'm Stuart, sorry." He stretched and yawned, "It's a small town, you never know."

Christ it's cold in Scotland, he thought as he approached the castle esplanade. He stopped and lit a cigarette, a habit he'd picked up in France - "Hey, it's de rigueur," he chuckled at his own joke. He'd try that one again later. He took in the expanse of concrete leading up to the castle gates; the bulk of the castle casting its protective shadow over the mob of tourists heading down the esplanade. He ruffled his hair, took a large drag on his cigarette, and in a moment he saw them both against the north fence. Euan in a black leather jacket, the rebel without a clue, and still as thin as ever. A bit thinner on top too by the looks of it. And Ian - knackered jeans and that same brown corduroy trucker jacket he'd been wearing for at least a decade. And what the hell was that on his face? A beard, untamed, he looked like a fucking tramp, the big ginger idiot.

A smile spread over his face as he approached. Ian and Euan broke off their conversation. "Evening ladies! Ian, what the hell is that on your face?" Ian rolled his eyes and they exchanged an awkward hug; Stuart didn't really go in for all that contact stuff. He turned to Euan, patting him on the shoulder, "Alright mate, how's the world of finance? Nobody smashed your windows yet?"

"Not yet, no. It'll come though. We were just saying how we knew you'd be late," Euan looked at his wrist, a retro LED digital watch showed the time: 17:07.

"Oh I'm so terribly sorry chaps," he hung his head in mock shame. "I've just been trapped in two rattling metal tubes filled with the rancid stench of other people's farts since 6:30 this fucking morning. Sorry if I'm a few minutes late."

"You could have flown," said Euan, instantly regretting it.

"That's not even funny you fucker. You know that'll never happen."

A travel writer with a fear of flying, Ian remembered. Still, he had good reason. He stretched his arms out and guided his friends by the shoulders, turning them to face Castlehill, the first stretch of the ribbon of history and culture that was Edinburgh's Royal Mile.

"Right, lads, all together now, let's get pished!"

CHAPTER TWO

Rosie

"No next of kin?" asked Fraser Urquhart over the top of his glasses.

"No, afraid not," said Rosie, shuffling through a bunch of A4 papers she'd placed on Fraser's green-leather topped desk. "There's nobody. There was a one-off payment in 1999, covered his stay here for 15 years, but there's no mention of who, or where, the money came from. All I know is he moved in here after his wife died. They didn't have any children."

Fraser nodded, "That's maybe not such a bad thing," he said. "With no relatives, there's less chance of anyone noticing he's missing. So he's never had any visitors?"

"None at all, not since I've been here anyway," said Rosie. She'd worked at the home for five years, straight from college in York, and had spent at least an hour or two of every day with Jock, perhaps seeing him as a surrogate for the grandfather she'd never known. "He's a lovely old man, but never sees a soul from outside the home. He's been happy enough, has plenty friends here, but he's never done anything like this."

"And nobody saw him wander off?"

"I've asked everyone, he hasn't been seen since lunchtime. I gave him his tablets at twelve o'clock, then walked him down to the dining room. He had some soup then said he was going back to his room. Look, Fraser, my main worry is that he's left without his medication. He needs to take this every three hours, and it's now," she checked her watch, "half past three. We need to phone the police!"

"Hold your horses there Rosie," said Fraser, chewing on the end of a pencil, "let's look at this carefully. We've lost a ninety-five year old man, a paying guest of ours, a fortnight before the inspectors show up. Doesn't look too good does it?"

"Well, no..." Rosie had to agree. Although disagreeing with Fraser Urquhart wasn't something she was afraid to do, so she continued. "But, regardless of that, we have a duty of care, and as he's paid up until the end of the month, we're still contractually obliged to provide that care. And one element of that care is ensuring we keep shoving his bloody tablets down his throat." She cleared her throat, "Wouldn't you agree?"

Fraser laughed this off. "I would Rosie, if we were looking at this in a purely contractual sense, but I say we give him a chance to return. This isn't a prison, he's free to come and go as he pleases."

"Yes but it's so out of character," Rosie argued. "He's never gone any further than the front gate in fifteen years."

"Well, maybe he just fancied a walk?" said Fraser. "Did he take a jacket? Or money?"

"No idea. I don't even know if he's got any money," said Rosie. "He does keep an old wooden box in his bedside cabinet but it's locked. We can't get into it."

"And you say he's only paid until the end of the month?"

"Yes, I'd mentioned it to him. He said he was going to sort it out - I assumed either he's got more money squirrelled away or he's got a mystery benefactor somewhere. There's a note in his file, just says..." she scanned the paperwork, "...paid in full.

Cash. Until end-September 2014. You signed it yourself."

"Yes I remember that day well," said Fraser, "it was very unusual, but we've never been in a position to turn down a cash payment of·well over £150,000. He arrived with his suitcase and handed over a large brown envelope. A room had just become available that very day. In fact, I think the ambulance had just driven off about half an hour before old Jock showed up. So that was that. He was in, and the poor old sods on the waiting list weren't to know," he chuckled. "He's not showing any signs of senility is he? Still got all his marbles?"

"As far as I know, yes. He's fine." said Rosie.

Fraser stood up and looked out the large bay window at the perfectly manicured lawn. Urquhart House was nestled in the heart of Marchmont, one of Edinburgh's more exclusive residential areas. His guests were happy here, he could see that. Some were out enjoying the afternoon sun, others were having a sing-song in the lounge. It may have been known as 'God's waiting room,' but he was providing as pleasant a passage into the afterlife as possible. The guests enjoyed it, and their offspring were equally delighted. It meant they didn't have to wipe their parents' arses after all, and they were willing to pay a premium for that.

"Okay Rosie, I say we wait for a while, then if he hasn't wandered back in by say, 10pm, we can report him missing. I'm convinced he's just gone for a walk." He turned from the window and looked Rosie straight in the eye, "We can't risk any bad publicity here. We'll lose our standing. We're one of the finest rest homes in Edinburgh, with a reputation to maintain. If we lose that, we lose the ability to charge the old buggers through the nose for their care. And if that happens, who knows? In this climate, it'd probably mean, what do they call it now? Downsizing? None of us want that." He held Rosie's gaze to make sure she'd understood the threat. "So, can I have your word you'll keep quiet about this, at least until tonight?"

Rosie thought for a moment, sighed, and said, "Yes Fraser, of course." Hopefully her eyes didn't betray what she was really thinking.

Rosie ran down the corridor. The nameplate on the door said: 'Room 51, John (Jock) Smith'. It was at the end of the west wing, looking out over the small garden to the side of Urquhart House.

The door was open. They had a 'no locked doors' policy. Always safer when your guests were likely to require urgent medical attention at a moment's notice.

Inside, the room was as she'd left it earlier. She looked around for any clues, any indication of what he might have been up to, or where he had gone, but could see nothing. His slippers were by the bed, his dressing gown hanging on the back of the door. Jock kept a very tidy room, and the sparse decoration didn't leave much space for hiding things. On a chest of drawers was a picture of Jock and Ellie, his wife. By the looks of it, it was taken relatively recently. Must have been not long before Ellie died in 1999. They stood together, huddled close, with hills in the background and smiles all over their faces. Ellie must have been beautiful in her day, Rosie thought. Despite her age in the photograph, her eyes shone with life and humour. And her shoulder length hair blew over her face in a youthful mess, a bit like Rosie's actually. Maybe that's why Jock liked Rosie so much? He loved to talk about Ellie, and his eyes often welled-up as he reminisced to Rosie about their life together.

She knew they'd married after the war, but had never had children, and this weighed heavily on Jock. It saddened her too, if she was honest. They seemed like a couple who would have made great parents.

"Oh Jock!" she said, scanning the room, "where the heck are you?"

She'd already checked the old box in his bedside cabinet, but the combination padlock kept the contents a secret. She pulled out the box again. Shaking it gently, she could hear a shuffle from within. Could be money, she thought. Turning it over she saw an engraving on the base; a maker's mark she guessed: WB, 1759. "My God, this thing's ancient," she said, under her breath. Splitting the box open was no longer an option. She set it carefully on the bed and thumbed the dials on the padlock. Hmm, worth a try, she decided, and dialled in 1-7-5-9, but it stayed closed.

She ran her hands through her tangle of blonde hair and racked her brains for a clue. She remembered his birthday this year, she'd taken him some flowers to brighten his room, and he'd just taken the box from his cabinet. It was 31st January. She was placing the flowers in a vase while he was busy with the box, opening it at the window and singing a song to himself. What was it? "Oh this is the year I was born..."

The year I was born? 1919, she knew that. He'd told her all about the day's events. Quite a day by all accounts. She sat on the bed and dialled in 1-9-1-9. The lock stayed shut. Okay, she thought, month and year, 0-1-1-9. Still locked. Day and month? 3-1-0-1. Still locked. Day and year? She was clutching at straws now. Dejectedly she dialled in 3-1-1-9. The box stayed locked.

She flopped back and stared at the ceiling. She couldn't let him just disappear like this. He needed his medication and she'd never be able to live with herself if he came to any harm as a result of missing his tablets. It was her job to make sure he took the bloody things.

What had Fraser asked? "Did he take a jacket?" - she opened the wardrobe and scanned the contents. He kept it very neat - a throwback to his army days. Shirts to the right, jumpers in the middle, trousers to the left. She ran her hands along the hangers - white shirts, blue v-neck jumpers, and grey flannel trousers - the standard attire of the Scottish pensioner. Everything seemed in place. Everything? That was odd though - there were no empty hangers. What had he been wearing at lunch? White shirt, grey flannels - nothing unusual, then it struck her - the hanger to the extreme left - Jock had kept his army trousers there - he wore them every year on Remembrance Sunday. They were gone. Red tartan trousers, his regimental tartan - replaced by the grey flannels he'd been wearing earlier.

Okay Jock, you've got all dressed up for something, but what?

She checked her watch, nearly four o'clock. She'd never bunked off early in her life but she was going to do it now. To hell with Fraser Urquhart.

Grabbing the picture of Jock and Ellie, she left the room and hurried to the staff room, where her friend Sheila was stirring a freshly made coffee.

"Graveyard shift?" asked Rosie.

"Yup," Sheila sighed, "Just preparing myself. I heard about Jock, poor sod. You want a cuppa?" she asked.

"No Sheila, not today," Rosie said, adding a hint of drama to her gentle Yorkshire brogue.

She took her yellow hiking jacket from a peg and wrestled herself into it, then unlocked the medicine cabinet and opened a drawer marked '51'. Pulling out two boxes of tablets, she checked the labels, placed one back in the drawer and stuck one in her jacket pocket.

"If Jock shows up, make sure he takes his tabs," she said, tapping the drawer.

Sheila sipped her coffee and nodded. "You're going on a Jock-hunt? Where are you going to start looking?"

"I've no idea Sheila, but I can't just sit here. If Fraser asks where I am, say I'm trying to save his reputation."

She headed out the main doors and bounded down the steps with purpose, but paused at the main gate.

Where the hell do I begin? she thought.

CHAPTER THREE

The Ensign Ewart

"This do?" said Ian as he moved to push open the door to The Ensign Ewart, the closest pub to the Castle. There was no point wasting valuable drinking time on indecision and treading the pavements, he thought.

"As good as any," said Euan.

"Suits me, I've never been in here," added Stuart.

The first thing that hits a drinker when entering a Scottish pub since the smoking ban is the smell of the punters. This late-afternoon, The Ensign Ewart avoided this affront to their senses by being almost completely empty, save for the barman and an old guy at the end of the bar. He glanced in their direction and, with a nod, raised his glass at them.

Ian smiled and nodded back.

The barman glanced up from his newspaper. Ian noticed the headline - "ON A KNIFE-EDGE" - referring to the most recent poll on the referendum. It was going to be close. There was nothing between the Yes and No camps now, and just a dwindling number of undecideds. He wished they'd make their fucking mind up. "What can I get you lads?"

Ian stepped up. "Pint of 80' please," then turned to Euan.

Euan scanned the bar and muttered, to Ian, "Ahhh, pint... of... Guinness... please Ian."

"Pint of Guinness," confirmed Ian to the barman.

"I'll have a lager," added Stuart.

The barman nodded and gathered three fresh glasses. For a moment, the only sound was the gurgle of the Guinness tap.

He turned to Euan, breaking the silence, "Guinness? Since when?"

"Aye, erm, just recently. I've not been drinking too much lately, I get pished too easily these days. It's a strategic move."

Ian glanced at Stuart, who looked similarly puzzled. "Eh? What's the strategy?"

Euan explained, "Well, truth is, I can't stand the stuff, so it takes me ages to drink. Therefore, I remain relatively sober."

Stuart looked at Ian momentarily, then joined him in laughter.

"Genius move," said Ian, shaking his head as the barman set three pints on the drip tray.

"There you go lads, enjoy," he said, glancing at Stuart with a nod towards Euan and a grin that said: "Who's your mate?"

"Cheers!" said Ian as they sat at a table by the window and clinked pint glasses. The head of Euan's Guinness spilled and ran over his wrist. He licked it clean with a "Eugh!" and a shudder.

"Euan, you are the weirdest individual I think I have the pleasure of knowing," Stuart said. "How long's that pint going to last you?"

"It won't take me any longer than yours, believe me. Problem was, I was hammering the stuff before. I'd have been halfway through a lager before your arse was even on that stool."

"Aye?" Stuart raised his eyebrows and looked at Ian, who leaned forward and stroked his beard.

"How so Euan?" said Ian, "You've always been the sensible one. That bank not been paying your bonuses on time or something?"

"Ach no, it's not money, I've got plenty of that, it's just..." he glanced up. The old man was shuffling past their table and was scanning the three of them with bright blue eyes. His stooped figure, supported by a grey aluminium walking stick, seemed to take an eternity to pass. Euan watched him head towards the toilet then decided the moment for explaining his problems could wait. "It's just, ach, nothing to worry about. I was getting a bit of a beer gut, that's all."

"Well, you've always been a skinny bastard," said Ian. "You must've looked like a bit of knotted string. Was Vicki giving you grief?"

"Nah," sighed Euan and gazed towards the bar. "Just trying to look after myself, that's all. Anyway, Stuart, how's France? I see you've been working on your tan. You not got yourself a fillie yet?"

"A horse?" asked Stuart.

"Is that not French for a woman?" said Euan, by way of explanation.

"It's 'fille' ya fanny," said Stuart, correcting the pronunciation. "And no is the answer. But aye, it's great. Been spending less and less time here to be honest. I'm still renting the flat in Portobello, but most of my stuff's over there."

Must be nice, thought Ian. It was common knowledge that Stuart had inherited an undisclosed sum after his father was killed in a helicopter accident when Stuart was halfway through his English degree. The helicopter had gone down in the North Sea on its way to the rigs - mechanical failure. His mother spent a large chunk of the compensation setting up an ill-advised dog-grooming salon in Buckie, but Stuart had certainly done alright out of it. He'd dropped out, bought the place in France, and had been drifting back and forwards ever since.

Stuart was filling them in on the renovation work. The place sounded pretty amazing. But did Ian envy him? Not really, he had Shona, and the kids, and nothing could top that. No matter how sunny it was, or how cheap the wine was. He envied Stuart's easy access to cash, but it wasn't like he hadn't suffered for it.

"...and I've got a regular bit of money coming in for the guidebook stuff, so, yeah, all's good. Planning to make the move permanently soon, to be honest."

Ian spluttered into his pint. With his beard covered in foam, he said, "What, and miss out on Scotland's glittering future! We're on the verge of freedom from Westminster for the first time in 300 years and you're fucking off to the sunshine? Traitor!"

"Ach you're not still banging on about that are you?" said Euan, taking another sip of Guinness and sitting back.

"I am indeed, as should you be. You still labouring under the illusion we're 'Better Together'?"

"I am, because we are!" argued Euan. "You still think we could survive on our own?"

"Of course we could, why the fuck not?"

Euan rolled his eyes and took a large slug of his Guinness, in preparation for the onslaught. He'd been expecting this, daft Ian and his crazy separatist ideas. Here we go.

Ian stared at Euan momentarily then continued, "I can't for the life of me understand why you think we can't. Look at Europe, at all the other supposedly 'small' countries - Norway, Sweden, Denmark - they all happily exist side-by-side, and survive. In fact they fucking thrive. They're already coming out of this fucking recession a lot quicker than we are."

"Are they?" Euan looked doubtful.

"Small ships are easier to turn around Euan." Ian said. "It's easier for them to adapt to change. Iceland's already halved unemployment, and what did they do? Bail out the bankers? Look after their friends in high places that fund their fucking election campaigns? No, they jailed the fuckers and invested in the people. Norway, discovered oil at the same time as us. Did they fritter it away like Westminster? No, they invested it in an oil fund that's now worth billions!" He took another drink. A bit early for this, he thought, but might as well strike while the iron's hot. "And look at Denmark, year after year, it tops the 'happiest fucking country in Europe' list. So what's so different about us?"

"We're never happy?" offered Stuart.

"Look at the taxes they pay over there though, they're fucking astronomical!" argued Euan.

Ian took another gulp of his pint, wiping his beard clean before continuing. "Yes, they may be. But did you hear the part about 'happiness'? Low tax doesn't equate to fucking happiness. I wish folk could get that into their thick fucking heads."

"No, but it helps," said Euan, "How the hell are you meant to survive if half your income disappears every month?"

"Because, dipshit, that money goes into paying for stuff that we're already screwed for in other ways. Childcare for one. It's all state-supported over there. I'm shelling out a third of my salary for Amy and Rory's nursery. And with another on the way, we're going to be fucked, seriously fucked. Shona can't go back to nursing full time, it's not worth it. I'm knocking my pan in, doing whatever I can, just to get through the month. High tax isn't a bad thing if it's making your lives easier and creating a fairer fucking society!"

"You're having another kid?" Stuart asked.

"Oh yeah, haven't told you yet. We are indeed. Shona can't get enough of this beard." He stroked the ginger tangle proudly.

"Rather her than me," said Stuart.

"Erm, aye well that goes for both of us!" laughed Ian.

Euan wanted to put an end to the politics as soon as they could. Get it over with now and they could enjoy the rest of the night. "Okay, what about other small countries - like Greece and Portugal, they're not exactly doing well are they?"

"Fucking corruption," said Ian. "And I tell you, if we had the people making the decisions just down the road, there's no fucking way they'd get away with any of that shit. We'd be down there, demanding heads on fucking sticks. As it should be. Accountable politicians. That's what independence means to me. We get the leaders WE elect, not the ones the South East of England want, and the fuckers are close enough that we can kick their fucking arses if they step out of line."

"So why aren't our friends in the south kicking the doors of Westminster down? People don't give a fuck Ian, keep the taxes low, keep the telly watchable, give us our two weeks in the sun every year. It's sad, I agree, but that's what we've become. It's what we're used to."

"I've got a theory about that," said Ian, "London's a big fucking doughnut. Get a round in and I'll enlighten you."

"Can't fucking wait," laughed Euan. "Same again?"

Euan got up and noticed the old man had returned from the toilet and was sitting a couple of tables away; hands laid on the table in front of him. He had no drink. He stared at Euan with piercing eyes. Christ he was fucking ancient, thought Euan. "You alright?" he asked. The old man nodded slowly, and a faint smile appeared through his craggy features. More noticeable in his eyes than anything. "Fine son, aye."

Euan returned with three pints and placed them carefully down. While at the bar, he'd been thinking about his next line for Ian, but Stuart was busy telling him about some five-star hotel he'd been reviewing. He listened for a while, taking it in. He was happy to be out of the house, with two of his best friends in the world. It'd been fifteen years since they'd left University, and five years since they'd last been out together. Why didn't they see each other more often? He knew the answer to that, but didn't really want to think about it.

He remembered those University days - they seemed like only yesterday. He'd completed a wholly uninspiring degree in Software Engineering. Ian had barely scraped through a History degree and Stuart had flunked out of his English course after losing his father. They were all fast-approaching 40 now, and despite two of them being married, were still living the extended adolescence that was so common amongst their peers. Maybe kids would have made the difference - he might have become like so many others at the bank. Settling down to a life of comfort, garden centres on a Sunday and The Daily Mail. But that wasn't to be. Even Ian, with his comfortable life, had his money problems. And Stuart, ever the dark horse, was he happy?

"...so aye, Champagne for breakfast, Foie Gras, and free slippers. Not bad at all. And I got paid for it!"

"Nice one," said Ian, glancing at Euan, who'd been lost in thought.

Euan seized the chance to butt in, "Right, William Wallace, if you think we can really manage on our own, explain the fucking mess of that city out there. Now, correct me if I'm wrong, but in eighteen-oatcake a few Irish blokes with pickaxes managed to lay tram lines spanning most of the city, and beyond. These days, with all the resources available to us, we can't do it without turning it into a majorly bureaucratic and fantastically inept balls-up that just about bankrupts us!"

They heard a snort. The old man turned to them from the next table and said, "Bankrupt?! Ye want to know about bankrupt? I'll tell ye about bankrupt son, if ye've got a minute or two?"

"Erm, aye, go on," said Euan.

"Right," said the old man, "ye might want to get another round in. Mine's a whisky, any kind."

Stuart stood up, "I'll get them."

He approached the bar. May as well humour the old guy,

he'd thought. He couldn't be bothered getting caught up in the middle of the independence argument, so the diversion was welcome. He couldn't give a fuck about it. He'd be in France next year anyway, so whatever they did in this shithole really didn't concern him.

"Four whiskies please, just cooking stuff."

The barman looked up from his paper, smiled, and pulled a bottle from the gantry.

"Don't suppose you could put some music on could you? It's a bit quiet in here," Stuart asked.

"Sure," said the barman, and pouring the whiskies with one hand, he reached with the other for an iPod that was wired into the pub's speaker system. He pressed play and set it down.

A familiar galloping bassline filled the room. Then the words "My My, at Waterloo Napoleon did surrender..."

"ABBA?" said Stuart with a raised eyebrow.

"Erm, aye, it's alphabetical. First thing that came on," said the barman. He held Stuart's gaze for a moment. "Here you go." He placed the four whiskies on the bar. He pointed at a jug and said, "There's water there, if you need it."

"Thanks," said Stuart, and handed over a twenty. Was that barman blushing?

Stuart placed the whiskies on the table, where the old man had now joined them. "Here you go. Sorry - what's your name?" he asked.

"Jock," the old man replied, and looked disapprovingly at the whisky, sniffing it while scowling at Stuart.

"Tight-fisted are ye?" he asked, and sighed, "Never mind. There's nae such thing as a bad whisky." Then, with a wink to Ian, "Some are better than others mind you."

He downed the whisky in one. "Come on then, are ye joining me or what?"

Ian shrugged and threw his whisky back, his throat burning and nose stinging with the warmth.

With a "Slainte" Stuart knocked his back.

Euan swirled his whisky around the glass, holding it up to the light.

"Oh for fuck's sake get it doon ye, it's no' a rare malt son. I've used better stuff tae clean shite aff my shoes!" said Jock.

Euan drank his whisky.

"Right, I couldnae help but overhear your conversation," began Jock. "And as there's naebody else in here for me tae bother, I thought I'd come and join ye. I hope ye don't mind - actually, I couldnae care less if ye mind or not. What I'm gonnae do, is give ye all a bit of advice. Take it fae an auld man, and take it tae heart..."

He paused, at first they thought for effect, but soon realised as he edged his backside onto one cheek, grimaced, and turned briefly red, that he was just preparing to fart, which he then did, loudly.

Euan sniggered into his Guinness. Then, remembering the crap Ian was spouting earlier said, "Hold on," and raised a hand at Jock. "Sorry, but before you continue we need to clear something up - London's a big fucking doughnut aye?" He pretended to hold a microphone under Ian's chin.

Ian cleared his throat for effect and leaned forward, tapping the imaginary microphone.

"What the fuck are ye doin'?" said Jock.

Ian continued, in a mock TV voice, "I do believe that London is a big fucking doughnut, yes. What successive UK governments have done is surround themselves with a big safety cushion. Like a big airbag of indifference. They exist at the centre of it, safely surrounded by a city's population that's been deliberately fragmented over the years. They've turned the working classes against each other, forced the middle classes out of the city and filled the void with immigrant workers, which I'm all for, but this has pushed the indigenous population to the outskirts, or the suburbs, or out of the city entirely. It's a deliberate ploy to keep the more politicised elements of the population at arm's length, thereby ensuring their safety. And that's why there's no fucking heads on sticks outside Westminster. Most of the population of London think it's just a big fucking clock!"

"I'm worried about you Ian, you're obsessed with heads on sticks," laughed Stuart.

Euan thought for a moment, "So in an independent Scotland, Edinburgh wouldn't be a doughnut?"

"No Euan, it'd be more like millionaire's shortbread. Layered, but solid, and tightly bound."

"With the toffee in the middle, is that the politicians?"

"No, that would be the people, holding it all together; the best bit. The shortbread base would be the solid foundations, the constitution, on which we'd build our new nation."

"So the chocolate on the top, that's the politicians?" asked Euan. He was loving this.

"Aye, exactly - exposed, so we can all see what they're up to, and they're the first bit to go. You can lick the chocolate off without affecting the caramel or shortbread underneath. And it's easily replaced."

"I love your Jamie Oliver school of politics Ian, I really do," laughed Euan.

Jock looked at them all open-mouthed and said, "Right ya daft bastards, are ye done?"

"Oh aye, sorry," said Ian, "you had a bit of advice for us. Do you want another whisky first?"

"Aye son, that'd be grand. And see if ye can spend a bit more than Rockerfeller here eh?" he gestured at Stuart.

While Ian was at the bar, Jock passed the time by drumming his fingers and staring at Euan. Euan did his best to ignore this, and asked Stuart some pressing questions about his train journey.

"Slept most of the way to be honest, once I'd managed to extract myself from the attentions of a pished-up divorcee."

"You always manage to pull, you handsome swine," laughed Euan.

"Erm, not on this occasion," Stuart said. "You should've seen her. Had a bit of a crisp problem, let's put it that way. Nice enough though; harmless. She was just being friendly, and let's face it, she's only human." Stuart flicked his fringe to one side, dramatically.

Euan raised an eyebrow, snorted, and took another drink of Guinness. A comparatively large one this time.

He'd always been envious of Stuart's looks - a black mop of hair fell over his tanned features. Girls had been falling over him at University, but as far as Euan could remember he never seemed to settle on one. Euan, on the other hand, had married the first woman who'd have him; Vicki, who he'd met at the first bank Christmas party he'd attended. He'd spent the entire evening by the canteen vending machines discussing with anyone who'd listen the dangers of updating the bank's ageing computer systems, which used an arcane programming language called COBOL. As the night progressed, his audience dwindled, and by midnight, he found himself alone, eyeing up the different soups available from the machines. She'd approached him, teetering on high heels she wasn't used to wearing and drunk on champagne she was, unfortunately as he'd later find out, very used to drinking and said "Get your coat baldy, you've pulled." The rest, as they say, was history. And not a very inspiring one.

Jock, still staring at Euan, was singing quietly now. Jesus Christ, he thought, we've picked up a right bampot here. Euan didn't recognise the tune, but the words seemed to be: "Oh why should I be so sad on my wedding day?"

Ian returned, placing four tumblers on the table. "Macallan alright?"

Jock stopped singing. "Oh aye, better," he said and drained

the glass.

He licked his lips, which were barely visible - lost in the folds of his craggy features. "Right, where was I?"

"Advice," said Ian. "You had a bit of advice for us."

His blue eyes lit up and he sat bolt upright in his chair. "Oh aye, that's right. Advice. Aye. What was it now?" He stared at the table.

They put down their drinks and waited. Outside, the commentary from an open-top tourist bus momentarily destroyed the silence.

Jock nodded to himself, then raised one finger, and with a pious expression, exclaimed:

"You must learn from the mistakes of the past."

This was delivered with as much gravity as he could muster, in that pronounced tone favoured by Glaswegian concert hall entertainers.

Ian looked at Euan. Stuart looked at Ian. They all turned to Jock.

"Is that it? Not sure it's worth two whiskies but aye, thanks," said Ian.

"Listen son!" continued Jock, leaning forward and tapping the table to punctuate his point, "I'll explain myself. My mistake was gambling. Yours might be something different, but mine was gambling. I lost every single fucking thing I owned on a horse. A fucking horse. If you can go away fae here tonight and promise me ye'll never make that simple mistake, my night won't have been wasted. Please trust an auld man. It's the Devil's work, gambling, but whatever happens in life, ye need tae learn from yer mistakes. Learn, and move on. Progress. Do ye get it?" He looked at them all in turn.

"Uhuh," said Euan, dismissively. Then took another long draw at his Guinness, admiring a large painting on the wall of a regiment on horseback, swords raised, charging towards him.

"How much did you lose?" asked Stuart.

"A lot," sighed Jock. "I was eighteen years auld. I sold everything for this one bet. Even cleared oot my mother and father's savings. I stood tae win a fortune, but I'd been lied to. The fucking nag was useless. Didnae even make it over the first fence."

Ian shook his head, "Who were you getting your tips from?"

Jock dismissed this with, "Och, a parcel o' rogues, that's all I'll say."

Euan looked down from the painting, "What was the horse called?"

"No' that it matters a jot," said Jock, annoyed, "but it was a useless bag o' glue called Caledonia." He gazed past Euan, his eyes settling on the door. "But that was that, I've never gambled a penny since. It took losing everything tae realise what a fucking idiot I was. I had my heid in the clouds. Eighteen years auld, and a total dreamer. But when that moment came, I saw the light, and I knew that the only way back was to beat them at their own game. Ye see, I'd learned fae my mistake."

"So what did you do?" asked Ian, draining the last of his pint and waving the empty glass at Euan.

"I became the bookmaker of course. I set up a card den, a poker club, ran it fae the back room o' a pub near St Giles, just down the road there," he indicated with a wave of his hand. "Exclusive membership. Lawyers, doctors, that sort ye ken? More money than sense. Well, soon enough I'd made back everything I'd lost, ach hell, more than that. There's nae harm in you knowing. In two years I made about four hundred thousand pounds. Some of them had ran out o' money and were paying me wi' fucking shite they had lying about their houses. That's when I decided it was time to get out. The way I saw it, it was compensation for my gambling disaster. God, or someone, was looking out for me. I shut up the shop. As far as I could see, I was set for life."

Stuart, seeing some parallels with his own situation, chipped in, "And were you?"

Jock lifted his empty glass, "No, because some bastard called Hitler invaded Poland!" He held the tumbler towards Euan.

Euan drained the last of his Guinness. He wasn't sure he had the energy to listen to Jock's tales all night. The three of them hadn't been together for five years after all, and they had a lot of talking pish to do. "Will we get another here, or move on?"

"You're no' gonnae make an auld man walk are ye?" asked Jock. Then, "Oh, haud on, I get it. You're moving on without me. Aye okay, away ye go then. I'll just take my place at the bar. Alone." He looked at the ceiling with watery eyes.

"Don't be daft, you're coming with us," said Ian. This old guy was good company. Another couple of drinks and he'd probably bail out anyway. The night was young, after all. Plenty time to work on Euan's political weaknesses yet.

"Ach go on then," said Jock with a smile. "Wait for me though, I need a pish. And I've got something I need tae do."

Euan looked at his friends, shook his head, and reached for his pocket as his mobile phone chirped.

Stuart watched Jock shuffle off to the toilet then looked at Ian and laughed, "What a guy eh? Think it's all true?"

"No reason why it wouldn't be," shrugged Ian. "And knowing how crap your chat can be, I for one am looking forward to his company."

"What's with the red tartan breeks? He'll be telling us he was the original singer for the Sex Pistols next."

"I think that's a Royal Stuart tartan," said Ian. "My cousin got married in that. Is that the wife checking up on you Euan?" he said, nodding at Euan's phone.

Euan sighed, "Aye, you could say that." He shoved the phone back into his inside pocket. "Right, a couple more drinks then we ditch grandad aye?" Euan was uncomfortable around Jock. The staring, the singing. Why did he always attract the nutters?

They were milling around at the door when Jock emerged from the toilet. "Give me another minute lads," he said and headed back to the bar. "Highland Park please Robert, 18 years."

Euan said, "I thought we were leaving? Is he buying us one?" Jock handed the barman some coins.

"Nope, doesn't look like it," said Ian, leafing through a discarded copy of The Racing Post.

"And he called me tight?" said Stuart.

Jock took his whisky to one wall, where there were two crossed swords among a cluster of pictures, raised his glass and said, "Second to none, Charles, second to none."

He drained his glass, turned and said, "Right lads, where's next?"

"Erm, Deacon Brodie's do?" offered Ian. Euan and Stuart nodded.

"Who's Charles?" asked Stuart.

"Oh, just a brother o' mine," said Jock, "An old brother. Lead on MacDuff." He opened his arms towards the door.

CHAPTER FOUR

Rosie

Standing at the gates of Urquhart House Rosie was hit by the realisation that she had absolutely nothing to go on. Other than the fact he'd put on his regimental trousers, Jock had left no indication of what he was up to or where he'd gone.

She scanned the street in both directions - away from town, into the upmarket residential south-side, and into town, towards the Meadows, which would be busy now with sun-bathing students. Jock was the type of person to seek out people and life, she thought - he loved to talk and tell his daft stories - so on a hunch, she headed towards the Meadows.

She stopped every passer-by and showed them the picture of Jock and Ellie but nobody could offer her anything but shrugs and apologies. She tried the nearby shops, but he hadn't been seen in any of them. The local pub drew a blank too, since it had been given a recent makeover and cursed with an unpronounceable name, she didn't think Jock would have set foot in the place.

She was at the edge of the Meadows now, acres of greenery spread in front of her with the rectangular glass peaks of the old hospital redevelopment catching the sun behind.

He could be anywhere, she thought. Her eyes scanned the Meadows for a small stooped figure wearing tartan trousers but there was no sign of him. She flopped on a bench and looked again at the photo.

"Where are you Jock? Where are you!!!?" She held it up in front of her, gripping the frame in both hands and shaking it in frustration.

She lowered the photo and stared straight ahead at an old police box, now converted into a small coffee hut. They'd done this with loads of the old police boxes in town. Totally ruined the "Tardis" thing for kids, she thought. The barista sat staring out, bored. Not a lot of coffee buyers today, it being a hot autumn day. She had an idea.

"Have you seen this man?" she asked the barista, who was suddenly delighted to have someone to talk to. "He was wearing red tartan trousers."

"I have yes," she said, in accented English. "He passed here earlier today. I thought he looked very smart in his trousers. I stare out a lot. Nobody buys coffee in this weather."

Rosie couldn't contain her joy. "When did you see him! Which way did he go?"

"Oh long time ago, about half-past twelve, maybe one o'clock?" Rosie checked her watch, half-past four now, damn. "He headed up there." She pointed up Middle Meadow Walk. The direct path into town.

"Thank you so much," said Rosie. She was about to leave, but thinking she'd better show some gratitude said, "Oh, I'll take a coffee please, whatever's quickest."

"Espresso?"

"Yes, that's fine." She counted out the exact change and dropped it on the counter. Then dropped another 50p into the cup marked 'Tips'. It was a start, she thought. And there was another one of these coffee booths at the other end of the path.

She'd maybe strike lucky there too!

The barista presented a tiny cup of black espresso and Rosie downed it in one, burning her throat in the process, "Ouch! Thanks again!"

She set off up Middle Meadow Walk, walking quickly past the dawdling students and occasionally jumping out of the way of a speeding cyclist. The sunlight dappled the path ahead, the shade of the trees keeping her cool as she powered onwards.

So Jock, you're heading into town - regimental trousers on. Was there a military parade today? She didn't think so, and if he'd wanted to attend it he could have asked. She'd have filled out the paperwork and arranged a chaperone. No, it must have been another reason. A re-union maybe? But why leave without asking permission? What was he up to?

The peace of the Meadows gradually diminished as she approached the end of Middle Meadow Walk, emerging into the bustle of the city. Buses negotiated the tight corner into Forrest Road and headed into town. She spotted a coffee booth, staffed by another bored looking Eastern European, lured to the UK by the false promise of a better life.

She approached the booth and held up the photo. "Hello. Did this man pass by here today, around lunchtime? He was wearing red tartan trousers."

The barista looked at it and laughed. "Yes, I saw him. He's a crazy guy! He was, what's the word..." she paused, "...fighting with a bus."

"Fighting? With a bus? He's ninety-five years old!" Rosie looked confused.

"Not fighting, sorry, arguing. Yes. He was crossing the road, and a bus was, you know," she made a honking noise, "and this old man dropped his things on the road. He was shouting at the bus, waving his stick at the driver. It was very funny."

"Did you see what he dropped?"

"Yes, it was a book and..." she looked upwards, searching for the word, and mimed pinning something on her shirt. "Medals, yes, it looked like medals. Lots of them. He picked them up and wrapped them in his newspaper then headed off up there." She pointed up Forrest Road, towards the city centre.

"Thank you so much," said Rosie. Then, "Oh, I'll take an espresso." She wished she didn't feel so guilty about things all the time.

"No problem," said the girl, placing a small paper cup under the machine and cranking the handle. "He must be a very brave man, with all those medals."

Yes, thought Rosie, counting out some change. He must be a very brave man indeed.

She downed the espresso and stared towards Forrest Road. Heading into town then Jock, what are you up to?

Rosie hurried towards the sandstone bulk of the National Museum of Scotland. She'd spent many a happy Sunday afternoon here since moving to Edinburgh. She always managed to get lost in the new building, and thought it was incredible how they'd managed to jam so much into such a small space. She'd seen old photographs, and it had just been an uninspiring square of grass before, looked over by Greyfriars Bobby across the road. The little statue of a dog that was such a magnet for tourists.

That little dog would be no use to her today though. She needed a clue. Maybe Jock was taking his medals to the museum? It was a possibility. She headed for the entrance.

"Spare some change please?" A homeless man, in his forties sat cross-legged on the pavement with a bedraggled looking dog sleeping alongside. He held a card saying: "Ex Army. Homeless and Hungry. Please Help."

"Of course, just a sec," Rosie reached into her pocket and pulled out a pound coin. "Here you go."

"Thanks. I've been sitting here all day and you're only the

second person to give me anything." He looked at her with gratitude. "You're a good person, have a nice day." He coughed.

"Thank you - you too," said Rosie, then stopped. No harm in asking, she pulled the photo from her jacket, "I don't suppose you've seen this man? He passed here earlier today. Ninety-five years old, red tartan trousers?"

"I have aye," said the man. "He was the other person. Gave me this," he reached under his backside and pulled something out. "It's no fucking use to me like, but he said I could sell it." He held up an old leather-bound book. Rosie took it and looked at the spine - 'The Wealth of Nations, by Adam Smith.' She flipped it open, looking for clues. 'An Inquiry into the Nature and Causes of the Wealth of Nations', she read on and gulped at the date, 'MDCCLXXVI'. That's almost as old as Jock's old treasure box, she thought.

She closed the book carefully. "Did you see which way he went?"

"Better than that. He told me where he was going. The Castle. Had some business there." He coughed again.

Rosie's eyes lit up. "Oh my god, thank you, thank you, thank you!" She knelt and grabbed the man by the shoulders. "You look after yourself now. And look after this book," she placed it carefully in his hands. "I've got a feeling it's worth a lot of money. There's an antique bookseller just down the road there. I'd suggest you go for a little walk."

"Eh, this thing?" said the man, looking at the book in his hands. "I've been sitting on it. Keeps my arse off the pavement."

CHAPTER FIVE

Deacon Brodie's

Euan and Stuart arrived at Deacon Brodie's first, Ian straggling behind with Jock. There was a crowd of smokers outside - mostly young guys, some in poorly fitting suits, some in jeans and t-shirts. They seemed to be in a buoyant mood, laughing and chatting loudly.

"Looks a bit busier in here anyway," said Stuart, taking a last drag on a cigarette and stubbing it out in a flowerpot.

Euan looked back up the Lawnmarket for Ian and Jock. He saw them, just past the cluster of cashmere and woollen tourist shops. His eyes were drawn up towards the huge blackened gothic spire of The Tollbooth Kirk, towering over everything. This was now the home to the Edinburgh International Festival, and Vicki had dragged him there to some god-awful performance of a Shakespeare play a couple of years ago. He'd hated it. He wasn't even sure she'd enjoyed it. Neither of them had understood it, that's for sure. They'd ended the night arguing on the pavement outside before she jumped into a cab and left him standing there. He remembered that long walk home, the chill in the air mirroring the coldness that was beginning to encircle his heart.

"Come on," said Stuart, "we'll get the round in."

In contrast to the emptiness of The Ensign Ewart, Deacon Brodie's was rammed. They edged their way through the crush to the bar.

"Jesus, busy in here eh?" said Stuart to the barmaid when they finally made it through.

"Big court case across the road, just got out," said the barmaid, then added, as quietly as she could against the din, "a few nutters among them, so watch yourself."

Stuart got the drinks in. Three pints, and a whisky for Jock. A Balvenie this time.

"So what were you going to tell us about earlier?" asked Stuart, "before old farty-pants joined us?"

Euan took a long drink of Guinness then wiped his lip. Bolstered by the alcohol now, he sighed and said, "My wife's having an affair." He looked at Stuart, deadpan, to make sure he knew this wasn't a setup for another crap joke.

Stuart was stunned. He'd never had much time for Vicki, but the guy didn't deserve this. "Christ! Sorry to hear that. Has it been going on long? How did it, erm, who is it?"

Euan shook his head, "It's hard to know where to begin."

There was a huge cheer from the entrance. "I'll tell you later," Euan said as he turned to the noise.

Ian and Jock had arrived, and the cheer had gone up from the bunch of smokers at the door. One was doing a poor attempt at a highland dance while the others laughed and clapped in time. This appeared to be directed at Jock. Euan looked at them a bit more closely now. They were all skinny wee runts, most with shaved heads but one or two with those ridiculous little fringes kids had these days, sticking up at odd angles with hair gel. Most were drinking brightly coloured alcopops, the starter drink of choice for Scottish neds, setting them up nicely for alcoholism and diabetes in later life. Another burden on the health service and the welfare state. More of his hard-earned tax money wasted. This was the Scotland Euan saw only too often, not the romanticised vision Ian saw through his tartan-tinted glasses.

From behind him a woman's voice, rough with years of smoking, said "Hahaha, look at this daft auld bastard comin' in."

Euan turned and gave her a look. She was forced into a cheap looking black and white two piece outfit, which, with her orange face, gave her the look of a swollen belisha beacon.

"That daft old bastard's with us," he said. "Have a bit of respect eh?"

"Oh fuck off baldy, we're just havin' a laugh eh?" She turned back to the group she was with. More of the same. Rough looking fuckers, Euan thought.

"Christ what a bunch of dickheads eh?" said Euan as Ian finally managed to steer Jock through the crowd. Some were still pointing and laughing at Jock's tartan trousers.

"Who? These lads?" said Jock. "Ach they're just young. Ignore them. Were ye never young and daft yerself?"

"I'm not sure I was," said Euan.

"Do you wear them all the time?" asked Stuart, nodding towards Jock's trousers.

"No ya daft bastard. These are my regimental trousers. I had stuff tae do today. Some things require ye tae wear clothes appropriate tae the situation."

"True," said Euan, "I imagine most of the crowd in here are more used to wearing fucking shell-suits."

"Now now Euan," said Ian, "they didn't choose to be born into poverty."

"Oh here we go, the bleeding heart." Euan rolled his eyes. "So in your independent Scotland, what would we do with these fuckers? They're not interested in working, they'd rather batter some poor granny unconscious and help themselves to her purse. That's a day in the office for scum like this."

Stuart handed Jock his whisky as he moved to lean on the bar, hanging his walking stick on the bar's edge. "Christ that walk fair took it out o' me. Let me lean here for a bit."

"No bother," said Stuart, "I got you a Balvenie this time, is that alright?"

Jock's face creased into a smile, "Och aye son, much better. See, yer learning..." He licked his lips and drained the whisky in one. "Christ I've no' been in here for years," he said, looking around the bar.

"One of your old haunts?" asked Stuart.

"Aye, well, one of the boys fae my card school hung aboot here. I took the bugger for every penny he had." He laughed at the memory.

Ian was determined to chip away at Euan until he'd converted the misguided wee fool to his cause. He took a mouthful of 80' then began. "Look, I'm not claiming everything would be fucking rosy overnight, I'm not that daft, or naive, but we're potentially one of the richest countries in the world. If we keep our hands on our own wealth, we could wipe out poverty, provide jobs, and give these fuckers a bit of hope."

"And where does all that money come from? We're already relying on handouts from Westminster. I'd rather the mugs down south subsidised these feckless bastards' existence than it all coming out of our pockets."

"That's a fucking myth Euan, utter bollocks. We put in a lot more than we take out. A lot more. Do you actually believe the shite the papers are feeding you? Have you paid any attention during this campaign or are you happy to accept the view served up by the establishment? Don't you think they've got a fucking agenda? You're not daft man, we're sitting on trillions of pounds of oil and gas for a start."

"Aha, and what happens when the oil runs out? Where does

that leave us?" Euan argued, satisfied that he'd had the last word. He took a drink of his pint.

"I've got news for you Euan. The oil's going to run out whether we're part of the union or not."

"So you admit it, we're fucked?" said Euan.

"We're fucked if we don't do something now, that's for sure. If you really believe we're surviving on handouts, how do you think the bastards in Westminster will feel when they're not able to pilfer our oil money? Why do you think they're so desperate to keep the union? Out of the kindness of their hearts? It's because Scotland's where all the fucking wealth is! They've got fuck all down there, other than fucking call-centres and the crooked financial sector. They need us, we don't need them." He stared at Euan. Was this sinking in? Was he even listening? "And when the oil runs out, do you think they're going to treat us nice then? We already get a fraction back of what we put in, so you can forgot all that shite they tell you about us being subsidised. When the oil runs out, we'll be getting fuck all back. We'll be nothing more than an unwanted, cold, wet and miserable fucking burden on them. Do you think the union will be so appealing to them then? No, we'll find ourselves forced into independence. And broke. Do you not think now's the time to take control of our wealth and use it to build a future on? Otherwise, we will be fucked. Totally."

Jock raised a finger and chipped in, "The Scots suffer the miserable and languishing condition of all places that depend on a remote seat of government."

Ian paused, pointed an open palm at Jock and said, "...aye, exactly. See?"

Euan sighed, he didn't have the energy for this. That last text message from Vicki had knocked the wind out of him. He zoned out of Ian's rant and checked his phone again.

The message read: "D staying here tonight. Be better if you stayed away. We need to talk tomorrow. V."

He knew what that talk would involve.

They'd married within a year. A lavish do in The George Hotel, attended by two hundred family and friends. Ian and Stuart among them. The rest, it has to be said, were mostly bank staff. But that was some day, he recalled. It rained non-stop, but they'd been happy then. He was sure of it.

Vicki still worked at the bank's head office, two flights above Euan. She swanned around in the marketing department, which basically involved spouting a load of hot air and attending countless meetings, while he toiled away on his PC, seeking out bugs in the code, writing new procedures and operating on old ones. Breathing life into the ageing beast of the bank's computer systems.

Ian was pointing at the ceiling, "...look, even the fucking roses up there have got more space than the thistles - they're all trapped in fancy fucking woodwork..."

Euan glanced up, the carved ceiling showed roses and thistles in equal measures, he thought.

The problem was, despite it all, he still felt like he loved her. At least he thought he did. Didn't he? They'd never had children. She did get pregnant, in the early days, but they'd agreed it was too early in the relationship so she'd had an abortion. A few years later they decided it might be time to start a family. Although the cracks were already beginning to show. Maybe they thought children would fill those cracks and keep their failing relationship together. They tried and tried, but her periods kept coming. Each one a bigger punch in the stomach than the last. Tests followed - Euan appeared to be okay, but it turned out there had been complications relating to her abortion, and she was told she'd never be able to have kids. That's when she'd started drinking. It wasn't long before he was doing the same.

They were masking the pain by getting drunk every night in that big, cold, empty flat. The TVs kept getting bigger, as their conversations got smaller and smaller. Soon they were barely talking at all. Just drinking, watching DVDs, and going to work. The guilt weighed on him, and he was certain it was the stress that caused most of his hair to abandon him. But was it just that guilt that kept them together? He was partly responsible for their situation, hadn't it been him who'd first suggested it was too soon for a baby? That they needed to have some fun first? She'd agreed, but then she had no way of knowing about the awful finality of their decision.

"...oil, fishing, farming, wind energy, renewables, tourism. This place is the most beautiful country on Earth for fucksake. Of course we'd survive." Ian was still talking.

Euan, not even listening now, nodded. "Aye okay, whatever. I'm sure you believe the figures you're presented with. Much like I trust the figures I want to believe in. We'll see what happens next week eh? No point in falling out about it."

"No, absolutely. As long as you vote Yes," joked Ian. He had to pause to get his breath back. That rant had fairly taken it out of him. "Anyway, what's up with you? Your face is tripping you."

Euan took another drink, then sighed, "I've just told Stuart - Vicki's having an affair."

Euan, just about to take a swig of his pint, paused with the glass at his lips then lowered it slowly, "Shiiiiiiiiiit, fuck, sorry man. I'm ranting away here and you're... fuck. Who with?"

"The appropriately named Dick," said Euan, looking at the floor. "He works for one of the advertising agencies the bank uses. They were working on a campaign together, and in the words of the problem pages: 'one thing led to another...'"

"Fuck. How long's it been going on?"

"Don't know, a few months, probably. We don't talk Ian. Everything's fucking shit." Euan's eyes were glazing over. "You've got Shona, and Rory and Amy all living in one wee flat, no disrespect, but it's fucking tiny, and you're so fucking good together. All of you. You're a lucky bastard, I hope you appreciate that?"

"Of course I do Euan - I mean, we could do with a house as big as yours," he laughed, and Euan smiled, "but aye, I know I'm lucky. It's the kids, they..." he paused, "well, they kind of make it all complete, you know. I'm sorry Euan."

Ian knew about the abortion, and the fact they couldn't have children - Euan had told him all this on their last drunken night out - but he'd no idea things were this bad. Vicki wasn't exactly a laugh-a-minute, which is why he didn't see much of Euan. They only lived about a mile apart after all. But these days, it was all couples and kids. Euan and Vicki didn't really fit with their social scene, and Shona and Vicki had never really hit it off.

He continued, shaking his head, "Fucking hell man, I'm gutted. What are you going to do? Are you staying with her? Obviously I'd say you could stay with us for a bit but we're rammed as it is. The kids' room barely has space for their bunk beds, and - "

"It's okay Ian, thanks, I'll be fine. You know, in a way, I can understand why she's done it. Dick's got a wee girl from a previous marriage. She's getting the family she wants." He took another drink, about a quarter of his pint disappeared in one gulp. He smiled a pale smile at Ian and said, "It's all over bar the shouting, as they say. Although the shouting started about two years ago. Ach, fuck it. Look, we're out here to enjoy ourselves, don't let my miserable situation drag you down. I'll be fine. Maybe we'll sort it out. Get the drinks in."

Ian patted Euan on the shoulder. "As long as you're okay. Another Guinness then?" he turned to the bar. "Who's that Stuart's talking to?"

Euan turned just in time to see Stuart raise his hands defensively and mouth, "Okay, sorry," to a young guy in a suit, who ran his finger quickly across his throat and shoved past him.

"Stuart, you okay? What the fuck was that about?" asked Ian.

"Oh nothing, just some arsehole I thought I knew. Turns out I didn't. Bit lairy in here tonight eh?" he laughed.

Jock was still leaning against the bar, and had bought himself another whisky. He can't half put them away, thought Ian. Must be indestructible. Ian squeezed in beside Jock and waved a twenty at the barmaid.

Euan was looking back towards the door, "Ohoh, check this one out."

Walking in was another suited, shaven headed, upstanding product of the welfare state. Bigger than the rest, both upwards and outwards, this one certainly didn't have the malnourished look of the others. A cry of "Bubbles!" went up from the assembled throng. Like a conquering hero, he swaggered into the bar, chewing cockily on gum.

"Wow, he sounds hard," Ian laughed, still trying to get the barmaid's attention.

"Maybe he drowns his victims in hot tubs?" suggested Stuart.

Bubbles was heading in their direction. Slaps on the back and various cries of: "We knew you'd walk," "The cunt deserved it." And, from one wag, "FREEDOM!" delivered in Mel Gibson Braveheart style.

"Come here my laddie!" Euan turned to see the orange-faced woman open her arms to welcome the new arrival in an embrace. She pushed him back to arm's length, which, given the length of her arms, wasn't that far, and added, "Now fucking stay out of bother, right? Or I'll stab ye!"

Laughter all round.

It's like being in the fucking monkey house at the zoo, thought Euan.

Bubbles looked at his mother, and said "I promise Ma'. I promise." He then revealed the origin of his nickname by tipping his head back and blowing a large pink bubble with his gum. It popped over his face. Some of the crowd laughed and a chant went up of "Bu-bbles, bu-bbles, bu-bbles, bu-bbles!"

His mother shouted, "Some fucker gonnae buy my laddie a drink then?"

"Jesus fucking Christ," Euan said to Ian, "Where's Richard Attenborough when you need him? Can somebody explain this species to me?"

Ian just shook his head, "One more pint, then we'll get the fuck out of here."

Stuart supped his pint and asked Jock if he was okay. The old man had been quiet since they'd arrived, gripping the edge of the bar with one hand as he downed his second whisky with the other.

"Oh aye son. Takes me a while tae recover fae a walk like that ye know?"

"Doesn't affect your thirst though eh?"

"No, ye're right there. Ye cannae get enough o' the water o' life down yer neck," he said, holding up his tumbler and letting out a rasping, croaky laugh.

Stuart wondered about this old man. Was he just your standard Edinburgh eccentric, putting on his best trousers for a night on the tiles? Or was there more to him? "So why the trousers? What are you doing in town? Feel free to tell me to mind my own business."

Jock looked at him for a moment and said "I'm looking for somebody, that's all." Then, straightening up, he said, "What's your story son? That young lad looked like he was gonnae stick a knife in ye there for a minute."

Stuart looked behind him, then turned back to Jock and said, "I met him in a pub one night, that's all. Said hello. He told me he'd no idea who I was. Which is bollocks. Probably just didn't want to be associated with us old boys eh?"

Jock didn't look convinced, but said "Auld? Aye, I wish I was as auld as you. I'm near three times your age son, at least, dinnae forget that. I've had more jobs in my life than you've had shites."

Stuart laughed, "You're probably right there, I've not exactly got my hands dirty."

"How's that?" asked Jock, with a raised eyebrow.

"Well, I lost my dad years back. My folks still lived in Buckie, that's where I grew up, and he worked on the rigs. He left one day to start his two weeks offshore but the helicopter he was in never made it." He stopped here for a drink, his mouth drying up. This story never got any easier to tell.

"I'm sorry tae hear that son. It's a tough life on the rigs. Ye're far too young tae have lost a father."

Stuart nodded, then added, "We got a decent pay off. No compensation really for the loss, but it helped me and my mum out. She got a dog grooming salon. I bought a place in France..."

Jock spluttered, "A what? A dog room in where?"

"Dog grooming," Stuart clarified. "It's a place folk take their dogs for haircuts, shampoos, nail trimming, that sort of stuff."

Jock just stared at him. "For fuck's sake, I've heard it all now. So you're doin' okay then aye? Plenty money still?"

"I'm fine," said Stuart, then went on to tell Jock about his plans to move to the Limousin next year.

But Jock was no longer listening.

Ian had just managed to attract the barmaid's attention but as he leant to place his order there was a scream from the crowd.

They turned to see Bubbles thrashing wildly, arms flailing. He crashed into Euan and sent his remaining Guinness flying. "For fuck's sake," cried Euan, shaking the spillage from his hands.

Bubbles' hands were on his throat, his eyes bulging out of his head.

His mother was screaming, "What the fuck! What is it?

Liam? LIAM?"

Ian shouted, "He's choking - out the way, give me room."

He grabbed Bubbles from behind as a circle cleared in the crowd.

"What the fuck's he doing?" one cried.

"He's fuckin' bummin' him," shouted another.

"Get aff him ya fuckin' poof." One of the crowd took a drunken swing at Ian, catching him weakly on the side of the face.

Ian spat, "For fuck's sake, he's fucking dying here. I'm helping him you stupid wee prick. Get back!"

Confusion in their eyes, Bubbles' mother shouted, "Gie the boy room. I've seen this on Holby City!"

Ian squeezed and lifted Bubbles around the gut, once, twice, three times. He was turning blue now, eyes still bulging, clutching at his throat. Shit, thought Ian. The basic Heimlich manoeuvre was as much as they'd taught him at the work's first-aid course.

"He's fucking choked on his bubble gum," Stuart said to Jock.

"That he has," said Jock, then, with a deep breath, "Right, out my way everyone. I'm a doctor. Ian, lie the laddie down."

Jock kneeled beside Bubbles, who was still flapping, but much less wildly now. His eyes were rolled completely back, revealing bloodshot whites. His mother was in tears. "Help him, please help him!"

Jock shouted, "Stuart, throw me a straw fae the bar. I need a knife. Who's got a knife!"

In an instant, there was a crush towards him as Bubbles' friends pulled a selection of blades from inside pockets and waistbands. A range of combat knives, a knuckleduster with a bladed edge and a stanley knife were thrust towards him.

"Christ I only need the one!" cried Jock, scanning the selection and choosing one of the combat knives.

A collective gasp, several FUCKs, and a few screams went up as Jock ran the blade across Bubbles' throat and thrust the straw in the hole. Blood splattered onto Jock's white shirt as he leaned towards the straw. He smiled as he heard a hissing sound. The air rushed into Bubbles' lungs.

"Ambulance is on its way!" shouted the barmaid.

Bubbles stopped thrashing and seemed to regain control over his eyes. They rolled back into position, terrified pupils dilated. He looked at his mother who fell to her knees and hugged him, "Liam, son, can ye breathe?" She looked in horror at the straw sticking out of his throat.

"He'll be fine," said Jock, then, "Fuckin' help me up somebody."

Ian and Euan grabbed Jock under the arms and helped him to his feet. In the distance, they could hear a siren approach. The crowd gathered around Bubbles, who'd stopped thrashing and was nodding in response to his mother's questions.

"Did you just perform an emergency tracheotomy?" said Ian, jaw hanging open.

"I dinnae ken if that's what ye call it, but I'd seen it done in the desert. We were waiting for Rommel tae make a move, bored, and one of oor boys choked on a camel's bollock he was eating for a dare. The medic ran in, did what ye've just seen, and the boy was saved. Andy Gillies his name was, although he had tae live wi' the name 'Goolies' fae that day on. No' much worse than Bubbles here, really."

"So you're not a doctor?" asked Stuart.

"No, of course I'm no' a fucking doctor, but dae ye think they'd have let me save that boy's life if they'd thought different?" said Jock, tapping the side of his head. "Like I've told ye - ye learn as you go through life. Ye develop. Ye pick things up. That's what turns ye intae a man."

Ian and Stuart just looked at Jock, slack-jawed. "You're some man, Jock," laughed Ian, eventually. "I'll get that round in now, four quick malts aye? You've earned it."

Ian pulled the remaining notes from his pocket. Christ, only thirty quid left. And it was only quarter past seven. He knew what he had to do if they were going to make a night of it. He'd need to make a detour before they got to the next pub.

A crowd gathered around them, patting Jock's shoulders and shaking his hand as Bubbles was stretchered into an ambulance. The ned who'd taken a swing at Ian apologised and shook his hand. "Ye dinnae look like a poof, tae be honest. No' with that fuckin' beard." Bubbles' mother launched herself at Jock and hugged him tightly. "Thank you!" Her fake tan was streaked all over her face by tears. "I dinnae ken what else tae say. Ye've saved my boy's life. I need tae run, but let me buy you a drink." She waved a five pound note towards the barmaid, who was pouring four malts for Ian. "Hey, get him an Aftershock, and keep the change." She kissed Jock square on the lips, and ran for the door, followed by Bubbles' entourage, some still smiling back and giving Jock salutes and raised thumbs.

Jock stood there, looking flushed, but with a twinkle in his eye. The hero.

"You fought Rommel?" asked Euan, staring at Jock with new-found respect.

"That I did, aye. Knocked a hole in the side o' his tank myself. Chased the bastard halfway across the desert. We were the Scots Greys, The Dragoon Guards," he said, dramatically, "rode our tanks like horses and chased the panzers out of Africa. When we weren't chewing on camel bollocks that is."

Stuart and Euan looked at each other, grinning like idiots. Thoughts of ditching this old boy were abandoned. He was priceless. Euan reached for the Aftershock the barmaid had planted on the bar and handed it to Jock, "Here, you've earned this."

Jock looked at it with curiosity then took a sip. "What the fuck's this?" he spat, grimacing at the taste of it. "Tastes like fuckin' medicine. Here son, that's for you." He slid the Aftershock across the bar to Stuart who tipped it back.

"Thanks Jock. I think." said Stuart, gasping and shaking his head.

Ian pocketed his change and turned to them, "Here we go lads, enjoy!"

They drained four Laphroaigs.

Jock licked his lips and said, "Ah, that's better. Right, I'll get ye ootside, I need a pish again."

CHAPTER SIX

Rosie

Rosie checked her watch as she hurried up George IV bridge, dodging in and out of shoppers and tourists. Quarter to five now. The castle closed at 5pm, she was sure. Better pick up the pace. All that coffee had worked its magic and she was not only wired and focused, but was also desperate for a pee.

Her nerves on edge, she powered on. Luckily, her weekend pursuit of Munro bagging had given her the stamina and lungs of an ox. If only she had the bladder of one. She thought of last weekend's trip up Schiehallion - The Fairy Hill of the Caledonians. Jock had told her it was where they'd worked out the weight of the world. Something to do with the shape of the mountain and its remoteness. He was full of that stuff. Always bigging-up Scottish inventors and the likes. It was a lovely day, and a fairly easy climb, with amazing views at the top. You could practically see from coast-to-coast. It bothered her at first that other climbers were all in groups, chatting and sharing a hip flask at the summit. She didn't mind doing it alone. She liked her own company. Didn't she?

She sighed. Life in Edinburgh was wonderful, but she had to

admit she was lonely. Most of her conversations were with geriatrics, and while some, like Jock were witty and entertaining, others just rambled incoherent nonsense, cursed by dementia. One had claimed that Elvis had visited the home during the night, and swore that he stood in the lounge and sang, "Oh I love a lassie, a bonnie bonnie lassie she's as pure as the lily in the dell."

"Really?" Rosie had laughed, humouring the old dear. "Are you sure it wasn't the ghost of Andy Stewart?"

Why hadn't she met anyone? Her friends told her she was attractive, funny, and smart. Doesn't that tick all the boxes? The real reason was probably because she wasn't one for pubs and drinking. And in Scotland, that was pretty much all they seemed to do! She'd take the occasional gin and tonic, but she preferred long walks, and a nice cuppa when she got home.

God, don't think of coffee. She really needed to pee now.

She turned onto the Lawnmarket and headed towards Castlehill, crossing the road onto the sunny side. It was eight minutes to five. The pavements here were packed with tourists, milling around outside the cashmere shops and trying on those hilarious tartan hats with the red-hair hanging down the back. It was slow-going negotiating the crowd and she danced from side to side avoiding the crowds heading down from the castle.

She really was squirming now. Don't think about it, she thought. She passed a pub, The Ensign Ewart. She could just nip in for a quick pee. But what if they close the castle gates? No, she'd keep going.

She really was going against the tide now. Don't think of tides! The esplanade was busy, the mob of tourists mostly heading out of the castle and towards her, or standing in groups taking photos.

She imagined herself as a salmon, swimming upriver, but the thought of rushing water just made the pressing issue of her bladder even worse. And salmon don't wear yellow hiking jackets, she thought. She was thinking about anything now to take her mind off it. The coffee wasn't helping. Or was it? She broke into a run.

"Excuse me!" said a skinny man in a black leather jacket as she crashed into him. He was having as much trouble negotiating the crowd as she was, as he tried to head towards the north side of the esplanade.

She turned as she ran and shouted, "I'm sorry, I'm really sorry, I'm in such a hurry!"

He made a show of straightening his jacket, cricked his neck and walked onwards, towards a tall laughing figure with a ginger beard like a bird's nest. God I'm such an idiot. She thought.

"You're lucky, it's last entry at 5pm and I make it... 4.59pm... and fifty seconds," said the steward at the entrance, smiling and tapping his watch.

"TOILET!" she gasped.

"Erm, aye love, just through the portcullis, on your left. Castle closes at six you know, you'd be better coming back another day. The ticket office will be closing..."

But she was already through the portcullis.

The Japanese lady in the adjacent cubicle initially thought Historic Scotland must have been upgrading their loos in the high-tech style of her homeland as she heard a high-pressure stream of water from the other side of the divide. Like a garden hose filling a bucket. Although this was followed by a long and satisfied "aaaaaaaaaaaaaaaaaaaaaaaaah!" so perhaps it was just someone that had been really, really, desperate for a pee.

Emerging, relaxed and feeling somewhat triumphant, Rosie headed up the cobbled slope towards the inner gates. A steward stepped out, "last entry was 5pm I'm afraid. We close in an hour. Open again tomorrow though."

Rosie pulled out the photo of Jock and said, "It's okay, I don't want to visit. I'm looking for this man. He's a resident of the care home I work at, and he's gone missing. I think he had some business here today. He'd brought some medals."

The steward looked at the photo and shook his head. "Not sure, but I'll check for you." He stepped away and spoke into his walkie-talkie.

Rosie leaned against the wall to allow more tourists to pass. A young couple asked her to take a photograph. "Of course," she said and took the camera. She directed them to one side, to get the castle gates in the shot, then pressed the button. "There you go." She checked the photo on the display and handed the camera back. Another happy couple, she thought and breathed deeply.

"Right, good news and bad news," said the steward. "He was here, but he left a few hours ago, at about half past two according to the guy that was on the gate. He caused quite a stir. Lots of tourists wanting photos with him."

"What was he doing here, do you know?"

"Yes, he was visiting the regimental museum. The Scots Greys, up the hill." He pointed up the path into the castle, past the audio guide booth and the row of cannon. "On you go, I won't tell anyone." He made a show of looking around suspiciously, and ushered Rosie on with a nod.

At the museum Rosie found out from the young attendant that Jock had arrived in the afternoon, a bit out of breath, and said he "wanted to speak to the governor."

"Did he see him, or her?"

"Yes, he saw the curator - Major Macpherson. The old man was very insistent. I don't know what their meeting was about though, sorry."

"Can I speak to Major Macpherson?" asked Rosie.

"He's down at the National Museum just now; he had a meeting about lending some items to them. If you want to have a look around, he should be back soon."

Rosie called Sheila at the home. "Hi Sheila, it's Rosie. Has

Jock turned up yet?... No?... Okay, well I'm getting somewhere. He was at the castle this afternoon, long story, but I'm here now... Just waiting to speak to someone to see where he was headed after... If he shows up can you give me a call please? Ta. And remember he needs to take his tablets. Okay. Thanks Sheila."

Rosie wandered around the museum, looking for any sign of Jock in the displays. She knew he'd been a tank gunner, he'd told her that much, but there was nothing. He wasn't in any of the photos, as far as she could see, and she'd checked all the medals on display but his name wasn't alongside any of them. Where was this bloody Major?

After the third circuit of the museum she checked her watch, six o'clock. The assistant was turning off the lights in the display cabinets.

"I'm really sorry but I need to lock up now. Should've really closed half an hour ago."

"That's okay," Rosie sighed. "Thanks for keeping the place open for me. Do you think Mr Macpherson will be back today?" asked Rosie.

"He will be, I'm sure. These meetings can sometimes drag on a bit. If you know what I mean..." she waggled an imaginary glass to her lips. "You can wait outside. I'll tell security you've got an appointment."

Rosie smiled. Bloody great. The only person who can possibly tell me where Jock headed next, and he's going to be pissed.

"Thank you," she said and headed outside. The sudden brightness caused her to blink. She wandered slowly over the cobbles and took in the view. The early evening sun turned the sandstone of the New Town orange as it spread out towards the Forth. Punctuated here and there by clusters of dark green - the parks and gardens of the New Town.

She checked her phone again. No messages. Where was this mysterious Major Macpherson? Two old soldiers were leading her on a right merry goose chase. She thumbed through the photographs on her phone. Page after page of self-portraits taken at arm's length on the top of Scottish mountains. None of them really captured the splendour of the views. It was hard to get the perspective right when you were on your own. And she had that self-conscious face that most people had in pictures they'd taken of themselves. Trying to look noble, or mysterious, or angling their face to conceal a sagging chin. Rosie didn't have to do this, as her chin was nowhere near sagging. It was quite a fine chin, she thought. Like her fine nose. And nice eyes. She sighed again. Maybe she should try online dating? The thought of this terrified her though. Too many nutters out there.

She was snapped out of her thoughts by an odd humming noise and the sound of tyres on cobbles. Approaching her, at little more than a snail's pace, was an elderly, bespectacled man on one of those Segway scooters. It was struggling with the steepness of the slope and the cobbles. So much so that, after being stuck in the same position for about 10 seconds, with the motor screaming in objection, he stepped off and gave it a kick. He continued his journey towards Rosie on foot.

"Bloody thing," he said to her in passing, gesturing towards the Segway, "I live on a hill and I work on a hill. Thought it might help my old knees."

"Are you Major Macpherson?" asked Rosie.

He smiled and pushed his glasses up his nose. He looked Rosie up and down. "Yes, how can I help you?"

"I'm looking for Jock Smith, ninety-five years old. He came to see you earlier with some medals?"

"Yes, yes, he was here."

"Do you know where he was going after he left? I'm his carer, and I really need to get his medication to him."

"Let me think, yes, he said he was going for a drink with an old friend," was all the Major could offer.

"Did he say where?" asked Rosie.

"Afraid not," said the Major with a shake of the head. Would you like to see the medals, they're just in my office," he gestured towards the museum.

No harm in it, thought Rosie. She had nothing to go on now. And he'd left here hours ago. The trail had gone cold, so she may as well be polite. She'd head back to the home and wait. At least she knew he was okay. She'd call the police on the stroke of 10 pm if he hadn't returned. They'd be able to check the hundreds of pubs a lot quicker than she could on her own.

"Yes, okay, it'd be interesting to see what he was up to in the war. I knew he was a tank gunner but he never mentioned any medals."

The Major unlocked the door to the museum and flicked on the lights. "Wait here a minute dear. Can I get you a tea, or coffee?"

"Coffee, thanks, just milk."

He returned a few minutes later with a bundle of newspaper and two mugs of coffee.

"Okay," he said, "here we have them. Gunner John Smith, 'Jock' to his friends. Scots Greys, World War 2. Africa, Italy, France, Belgium and Germany. Got around a bit. And a bit of a war hero too by the looks of it. We're always grateful to receive donations, and he very kindly left us these."

He laid the paper out on a display case, opening it to reveal a cluster of medals. The brass or silver immaculate and shining in the museum spotlights. The ribbons similarly vivid, like they'd been locked away for years.

"Wow," said Rosie, "what were all these for?"

"Well you've got a fair few campaign medals here." He pointed out some of the medals. "These were medals you got for just 'showing up' at a particular scrap. He pointed them out in turn, explaining where and when they'd been awarded.

"But we've got a couple of crackers here." He set two medals aside. "The Military Medal, that's for bravery in the field." He tapped a silver circular medal with a red, white and blue ribbon. "And this one's the Distinguished Conduct Medal, again for gallantry." Another silver disc, with a blue and red ribbon.

She was amazed. He'd mostly joked about the war, telling daft stories about the lads he was with and the situations and scrapes they'd found themselves in. She'd no idea he was a bloody war hero.

The Major continued, "He's given us the medal cards. These tell us what the awards were for, if you'd like to read them."

She scanned the cards. The Military Medal was awarded in November 1942 in Africa. Jock had been involved in the capture of 300 prisoners and 11 artillery guns and had shown "Tremendous courage in single-handedly containing a large number of German troops."

Impressive, she thought. She tried to picture Jock as a 23 year old. It was hard to imagine the stooped old man she knew ever being that young, at least physically. Mentally though, it was easy. He had the same sharp wit as any of her friends. You never really get any older on the inside, she thought.

She picked up the next card and sipped her coffee. Distinguished Conduct Medal, December 1942, Africa again. A tank battle that had resulted in the capture of another 250 German prisoners. Jock had been praised for "steadfastness and tremendous courage, remaining in his crippled tank and continuing to fight while under fire, destroying two German panzers."

It was hard to connect this level of horror with the old man she walked slowly around the grounds at Urquhart House. Oh Jock, she thought. I really need to find you.

She knew she had to keep looking.

Rosie checked her watch as a security guard let her out of the castle. It was now after seven. The esplanade, more empty now, spread out in front of her. What chance did she have of finding

Jock now? At least she knew he was okay. He'd just wanted to hand in his medals, that was all. But why didn't he mention this? And why didn't he ask? She'd have filled out the form, packed his medication and arranged for a carer to go with him. She'd have done it herself if that arsehole Urquhart had let her.

She checked her phone again, no messages, she tried Sheila anyway.

"Hi, Sheila, no sign of Jock yet?... No.... It took ages in the museum, had to wait on some mad old curator arriving on a stand-up scooter. Must have reminded him of his cavalry days... Okay, no worries, I'll maybe have another hunt around but he could be anywhere. He's gone for a drink apparently... At least we know he's safe, but I'd still like to get his tablets to him... He left here at half two, so if he's gone to the pub for a couple of hours, he could still be hobbling back up the road to the home... Okay love, thanks. Call me if you hear anything. Bye."

While talking, she'd wandered over to the north side of the esplanade, and was now standing at a large stone memorial. She read the inscription "Here lies Ensign Ewart, Royal North British Dragoons." A great hero at the battle of Waterloo, it would appear. The stone had been placed by the men of the Royal Scots Greys. Jock's regiment. If only you could talk, Mr Ewart, she thought.

She gazed out over the view to the New Town, and beyond to the Forth, the grey-green band of Fife, and the distant mountains, just visible. She loved Edinburgh, and the way the city draped itself over and around its seven hills. She could get to those mountains in a few hours, but if that wasn't possible, there was always Arthur's Seat. What other city had a bloody great hill like that plonked in the middle?

She realised she was standing where the bloke with the ginger beard had been laughing at her collision with that little guy in the leather jacket. She laughed, what a bloody idiot you are Rosie! That little chap seemed nice though. She smiled at the memory of his sarcastic "Excuse me!" and the way he'd straightened his collar like Del Boy from Only Fools and Horses. He'd caught her eye, but she was so bloody bursting for a pee she had to keep running. Just my luck, she thought.

She shook herself back to the present. "Right Jock, I'll give it one last go, you old bugger."

She looked around, but there were no coffee booths up here. There was, however, an ice cream van, and she'd been lucky with her snack-selling sentinels so far.

"What can I get you love?"

Once again, Rosie felt obliged to spend money before asking a favour. "Oh, just a cone please, vanilla. I don't suppose you saw this man today did you?" She held up the photo. "He was wearing red tartan trousers. He's ninety-five."

The ice cream man presented her with a vanilla cone and leant onto the counter for a closer look.

"No love, sorry. This place is mobbed at this time of year. Only a few ways you can go though," he gestured to the top of Castlehill. "Either straight on down The Royal Mile, down the steps past Cannonball House, or down Ramsay Lane, but those might be a bit steep for an old fella."

"Yeah, I know. Do you know the pubs around here?"

"Drive my van up here every day love, I should do."

"Where do you think an old man would go for a drink, to meet a friend? Somewhere quiet probably, not too far?"

"Well you've got a few down there," he pointed towards Castlehill, "once you're past the Whisky place and The Hub, the big old church, you know?"

She nodded.

"There's the Jolly Judge, but The Ensign Ewart's the closest. If I was ninety-five, I wouldn't want to be walking too far."

The Ensign Ewart! The memorial! His regiment! An old friend, probably from his army days. Of course that's where they'd meet. And she remembered she'd considered going in there for a pee on her way up here.

"Thank you!" she cried, dropping her cone in her rush to leave. "Oh god, sorry, do you want me to..."

"It's okay love, the seagulls will get it."

Rosie barged through the doors of The Ensign Ewart at just after half-past seven. She was surprised to find, not a quiet pub as expected, but a heaving mass of tourists, all milling around taking photographs of the paintings on the wall, depicting the Battle of Waterloo.

She attempted to muscle her way to the bar.

"Excuse me could you take our photograph please?" an American voice, a woman in her fifties wearing a fawn jacket that perfectly matched her husband's.

"Of course," said Rosie. They positioned themselves in front of two crossed swords on the wall and smiled, presenting two sets of perfectly altered teeth. Rosie clicked the shutter and glanced at the photo. The flash had bounced back more off their teeth than the swords, but it would have to do.

"Here you go."

"Oh where are you from, you're not from round here are you?" said the man.

Rosie, impatient, but ever-polite, said, "no I'm from York."

"Oh York, we were there last week, beautiful city, beautiful."

"Yes, it is," said Rosie, looking around desperately for Jock. "I'm sorry, I really need to find someone," she smiled moving on through the crowd.

"Oh you'll find someone sweetheart," the woman said, "with those hips, are you kidding?"

Good grief, thought Rosie, but couldn't help a smile. She'd made it through to the bar and was trying to get the barman's attention but he was busy pouring pints while answering questions about single malt to another American tourist.

"Is this one peaty? I'm not sure I like the peaty stuff. Tastes like Germolene." asked the tourist, pointing at the whisky list.

"Yes, that one's very peaty. You might be better starting with an Oban, it's a wee bit west-coast, but not as in-your-face as the Islays."

"Okay I'll have an Oban. Honey, you want an Oban too?"

"Yes dear; Maisie, do you want an Oban?"

"Oh yes please, can you get Peter one too?"

"Okay, make that four Obans."

"We'll have an Oban too!" the couple she'd photographed shouted through the crowd.

"Six Obans," said the tourist. Then shouted, "Anybody else want an Oban?"

"I'll have an Oban," said an old man in glasses and a golf cap.

"Three Obans over here Jeff!" from another group at the window.

"Okay, ten Obans please, going once, going twice..."

"Who's drinking Oban?" a fat man in a denim jacket had just emerged from the toilet. "I'll have a double."

Bloody hell, thought Rosie, she frantically tried to get the barman's attention but he was doing his best to ignore her. "Excuse me!" she shouted.

"I'll be with you in a minute," he said, exasperated, as he pulled the bottle of Oban from the gantry and set out eleven glasses. He started measuring them out.

"I'm looking for someone," Rosie shouted up the bar. "An old man, ninety-five, red tartan trousers. Was he in here earlier?"

"There was an old man here yes, tartan trousers, came in about three o'clock. Left again about six."

"Was he with anyone?"

"Not when he came in, just sat and drank a few whiskies on his own. Big tipper like. But he joined a group of lads just after five. Sat and had a few drinks with them."

Rosie was worried, "What kind of lads?"

"Just three regular blokes, didn't look dodgy or anything.

One of them was bald, leather jacket, quite small. One had the worst looking ginger beard you've ever seen, like a tramp, and the other one was quite, well, loved himself a bit, I think. Dark hair, broody type." And bloody gorgeous, he thought to himself.

That sounds like two of the blokes I saw on the esplanade, Rosie thought.

"Any idea where they were heading?"

"I do, they said they were going to Deacon Brodie's. It's just down the road. Right, here we go sir, eleven Obans, this one's the double..."

Rosie was just heading out the door when she heard an American voice splutter, "How much!?"

CHAPTER SEVEN

The High Street

Outside Deacon Brodie's, they waited on Jock. The streets were still busy with tourists. The High Street, pedestrianised now, was a rolling sea of baseball hats, see-you-jimmy bunnets and day-glo kagouls.

Stuart wandered a few yards down the hill to light another cigarette. He read the story of Deacon Brodie mounted on the side of the pub. Born 1741, executed 1788. A cabinet maker by day, a burglar by night. We've all got our secrets, he thought, inhaling and looking back just as Jock stepped from the pub.

"Right lads, where's next?"

"We'll just keep heading down the mile," shrugged Ian. "No rush, a bit of a breather eh? We're not used to hammering it like you."

Jock laughed, "Ach get away. I've never trusted a man that doesnae drink. Come on, I'm thirsty." He stepped out onto the road and a taxi horn blared. Jock dismissed the driver with a shake of his stick and kept going.

"This boy's crazy," said Euan.

"I think he's great," said Ian, "and I'm dying to hear about his role in Hitler's downfall, come on."

They crossed with Jock, the traffic grinding to a halt at either side.

"There's no decent boozers on this stretch is there?" said Euan, as they made it to the safety of the pavement. They paused outside the High Court building at the statue of the philosopher David Hume. Jock was still crossing the road, shouting obscenities at a van driver.

"Hmm, not really. Could do with something to eat though," Ian said.

He stood, looking down the High Street through the crowds and absently rubbing the statue's giant toe, the brass shining under his finger and thumb.

"You got an exam coming up?" Euan asked. "Isn't that just lucky for philosophy students?"

"I'll take any luck I can get," said Ian.

Jock and Stuart joined them. "Right, keep going, once I get a head o' steam up, I'll be fine."

After a few yards they stopped. Jock was staring at a Charlie Chaplin mime, painted gold from head to foot. He approached and straightened up as much as he could to stare at the mime's face. "Hellllloooooo..." he said quietly. No response, so he stepped back. He turned to Ian, "What the fuck's this?"

Ian laughed, "It's a mime Jock. It's Edinburgh, the place is full of them."

"What does it do?" asked Jock.

"Just stands there, I suppose."

Jock turned back to the mime, leant forward and blew sharply up into his face. Still no response.

"This guy's good," Euan laughed. Stuart nodded in agreement. There was a crowd gathering around them now.

Jock turned, as if to walk away from the mime, then turned quickly. Staring him out this time.

Still nothing. The mime was as still as the statue of David

Hume.

Ian was about to hurry Jock along when, out of the blue, Jock swung his stick over his shoulder and took a swipe at the mime.

Charlie Chaplin leapt from his podium. Jock held the stick firmly in mid-air and burst into a cackling laugh, the crowd soon joined him.

"Here son," Jock said, tossing 20p into a tupperware box. "Ye've earned that."

The golden Chaplin gave an exaggerated bow and waddled back onto his podium. After he hopped up he stared wide-eyed at Ian and gave a sharp nod of the head, directing them down the High Street. Ian took that as mime-speak for "Please fuck off!"

They slowly made their way through the crowd. This stretch of the Royal Mile was a favourite haunt of performance artists, as well as being the meeting place for ghost tours and trips into Edinburgh's hidden underground city. Built over after the plague, before it was a tourist attraction - the council used to open it up to groups by appointment. Ian had been down there once, many years ago. He'd gathered a crowd from the office and booked them in. It was fairly atmospheric, but was spoiled a bit by the fact the council offices above were using it as extra storage, so the medieval vibe was shattered somewhat by banks of grey metal filing cabinets.

He hoped it'd be better now. He'd maybe take the kids one day, before the arrival of number three? He thought about Shona. She'd be getting them ready for bed now. Tucking them into their bunk beds and reading them a story. His heart swelled with love, as it was always more prone to do after a decent drink. But what the hell were they going to do in six months? The baby would be in their bedroom for a while, but they both knew they needed to move. It wasn't fair on the kids. They needed space to grow, to play, to develop, and more importantly, to stop them knocking hell out of each other for stealing toys, or breaking lego, or scribbling on each other's colouring books.

"Penny for your thoughts?" asked Jock. "You're miles away son, are ye drunk?"

"No," laughed Ian. He told Jock about the impending addition to his family and the sticky situation he was in. "Do you have children?" he asked.

"No son," Jock said, "that's one joy I've never known." He held onto Ian's arm for support as they walked. "You're a lucky man, I hope ye appreciate that? They're the greatest gift. The greatest..." He tailed off, looking down as he walked.

"Are you married?" asked Ian.

"I was married, aye," said Jock looking straight ahead now, "Ellie. A more beautiful lassie ye've never seen. Met her when we were on leave, getting ready for D-Day, and I married her as soon as I got hame again. But the children never came. For whatever reason, the stork kept missing our hoose..." He paused, took a deep breath and continued, "...and she passed away in 1999."

"Sorry to hear that," said Ian.

Jock walked for a bit, lost in thought, then continued, cheering up. "And that was when I realised I didnae ken how tae cook or clean a shirt so I took what money I had left and got myself intae a place up in Marchmont. A care home, ye ken? It's run by a total arsehole, but it's nice enough."

"So you're just on what? A wee day out? Are you allowed out?"

"Of course I'm allowed out! It's no' a fucking prison. The amount I'm paying them I'm entitled tae do as I like. Although, as far as I ken, you're no' meant tae just wander off withoot filling in a form or something. Anyway, that's naebody's concern. The reason I'm out, well one o' them, was that I wanted tae take some medals tae the regimental museum, up at the castle. I've nae children, so I thought they might as well have them."

"Medals?" Ian asked, "So you're a war hero too?"

"I wouldnae go that far," Jock said, eyes twinkling, "but I got involved in a few scrapes."

"We're going to get something to eat," Euan said, gesturing towards a chip shop. "Want anything?"

Ian looked around. "Aye, I do, but I don't fancy chips. I'm going to get something down the road, I'll get you back here in, what, fifteen minutes? You just want to wait here Jock?"

"Aye, nae bother, I'll just plonk my arse doon here." He eased himself down onto the steps at the foot of the Mercat Cross, St Giles cathedral towering above them.

Ian disappeared into the crowd and into the first bookmaker's he came across.

Ian stared up at the screens while checking through his pockets. That last round had left him with £14. He had his bank card, but he knew that withdrawing the last £40 of his overdraft would leave him screwed. It was two weeks until payday, and Amy had a birthday party to go to on Sunday so he'd need to buy a present tomorrow. Fucking hell. Shona knew only too well how skint they were, and to be fair, she managed to cut her cloth accordingly. Ian, on the other hand, was crap with money, and he knew it. The rounds of single malt whisky hadn't really helped.

He scanned through the displays for the next race. It was 19.40 here, there were no evening race meets, but there'd be something in the USA. There it was, 14.45 Belmont Park. He quickly studied the form, grabbed a betting slip and scribbled. "14.45 Belmont Park, £10 to win, St. Andrew @ 4/6"

A safe bet, on the favourite, and with a name like that, he couldn't lose.

It won.

Collecting his £16.67 he scanned the screens again. Next race was in five minutes, at another track.

This time, "14.50 Finger's Lake, £7 to win, Endeavour's Sail @ 7/4"

It won, he grinned at the cashier as he picked up his winnings. £19.25.

This gave him just under £40.00 in total. Could he ride his luck? He'd need at least fifty quid for another few rounds.

On the screen he saw it - 14.55, Aqueduct Racetrack. A horse called Independent Spirit. He checked the odds, even money. More risk, but he was on a roll.

"Not a bad fifteen minutes mate eh?" said the cashier as Ian gathered £52 from the counter. He pulled out the notes already in his pocket, the £14 he'd kept behind so if that last bet failed, he could walk out with what he'd arrived with.

£66, not bad, he thought. But every time he saw that number he was reminded of the fucking English and the World Cup win they would never, ever, shut up about.

As Ian worked his way back up the High Street he was aware that a crowd had gathered near the Mercat Cross, where he'd left Jock. His heart sank as he hurried through the crowd. Had something happened to him?

He needn't have bothered. Stuart and Euan were digging into bags of chips at the edge of the crowd, and up there, on the raised platform of the Mercat Cross, was Jock, waving his arms dramatically.

In the distant past, this was where proclamations were made, public shamings took place, and people were hanged. Jock was hopefully just performing some sort of proclamation, Ian thought as he arrived at Euan's side.

"What the fuck's he up to now?"

Euan grinned, eyebrows raised as far up his expansive forehead as they'd go, "He's on a roll. Got the crowd eating out his hands now."

"...and where are you from dear?" Jock boomed, pointing at

a dark-haired, middle-aged woman.

"France!" she shouted.

"And where do they make the important decisions for what happens in France?" He was using that Glasgow vaudeville voice again. All pronounced vowels and exaggerated facial expressions.

"In Paris," she said.

"Which is where? In France, if I'm not mistaken?"

"Of course," she laughed.

"And do you think it would be better if those decisions were made in Berlin? Or Madrid?"

"Of course not," she laughed again and shook her head.

"Of course not. And you sir, where are you from? You look cold. I'm guessing you're Italian, or Spanish?"

"Yes, I'm from Italy," the man laughed.

"Lovely place, went for a driving holiday there once. In a tank." Laughter rippled through the crowd, as explanations were hurriedly made in several European languages. "And when something vital to the wealth and security of your nation needs to be discussed, can I ask, is this discussed in Athens? Or in Vienna? No, I believe the decisions are made in Rome - beautiful Roma, am I correct?"

The man nodded.

Ian took a chip from Euan's bag. He pointed up at Jock and mouthed, "What the....?"

Jock continued his oratory, and Euan filled Ian in on recent events. "We just came out the chippy. Somebody from the Better Together campaign had stopped to ask Jock which way he'd be voting next week and he asked her to come back in a minute. That's her over there."

Ian looked where Euan was pointing to see a flustered woman in her forties with a clipboard. She was attempting to stop passers-by but nobody was interested, they all brushed her aside to join the expanding crowd around Jock.

"And you, the gentleman with the beard." Ian looked up to see that Jock was pointing directly at him. "You hail from...." he cupped his hand behind his ear, theatrically.

"Scotland!" Ian shouted, humouring Jock. What the hell was he up to now?

"And where are decisions pertinent to the running of Scotland taken, may I ask?"

"London!" shouted Ian, with a grin.

A boo went up from the crowd. Ian and Stuart were loving this. Stuart was laughing so hard several chips hadn't made it fully into his mouth and were gathered at his feet. Euan was shaking his head, but couldn't contain his smile. Jock calmed the crowd down, with two downward facing palms. A hush descended.

"And can I ask you all, where do you think decisions concerning the Scottish people should be made?"

"Edinburgh!" cried the crowd. Jock bowed theatrically, with a flourish of the hands. He'd learned that from Charlie Chaplin up the road. A cheer went up. Somebody shouted "Freedom!" and Jock descended to a round of applause, slaps on the back and many, many handshakes.

He hobbled towards them, numerous phone cameras filming him all the way, and the clapping crowd parting before him. He passed the Better Together campaigner, put his hand on her shoulder, and said, "I think ye know the answer now."

"Jock, does the SNP know about you?" Ian asked, grabbing Jock by both arms.

"I doubt that," Jock said. "Anyway, I wouldnae gie them the time o' day."

Euan looked puzzled. "Eh? After that speech?"

Jock just looked at Euan and said, "It's no' aboot party politics this son, it's aboot national pride. It's aboot Scotland growin' up and takin' its proper place in the world. It's spineless buggers like you that's the problem."

Euan was hurt by this, "I'm not fucking spineless. I just think it's too risky. There's too many unknowns. I don't believe the figures, and I think we're stronger as part of the fucking union, that's all!"

"The fucking union eh?" Jock winked at Ian, "he's learning…"

Ian grabbed another chip from Euan as they walked.

"Fuck off," Euan cried, pulling the bag away. "I thought you went for something to eat?"

"Erm, I did, aye, still hungry that's all. Tightwad. Hey Jock, didn't you say your old gambling club was around here?"

"Aye, it was," Jock said, looking around him, "That pub's no' here now though, I've nae idea what any o' these places are. Games Workshop, what the hell's that? Is that a card den?"

"Not really," Ian laughed, "although they do sell cards, of sorts. So what happened to the place? Did you just take all their money, wipe them all out?"

"Ach, just like I told ye, most o' my clients were rich, came fae the courts and offices and suchlike. I was quite a character in my day and word got around that there was a regular card game wi' high stakes. This was the years just before the war remember, there wisnae a lot of joy going around. We all knew another war was coming - it was just a matter o' when. So these boys were just happy tae have a distraction."

"And you were happy to take their money?" Ian smiled.

"Of course I was. Spread the wealth, that's my motto. Like I said, some o' them ran oot o' cash and started giving me stuff they had lying about their houses as payment."

"What sort of things?"

"Ach, books, antiques, that sort o' shite. Nae use to me at the time. I was twenty years auld, and just about tae be drafted. I stuck all my money and a couple o' bits and bobs in a safety deposit box in the bank, and that was that. I was away tae basic training. Next thing I knew I was on a boat tae Africa."

Ian, feeling warm and fuzzy with the drink, just looked in total admiration at this ninety-five year old wonder. What a life he'd had. What a life he was having. What a speaker. What a drinker. What a charmer.

"Where's the next bloody pub," Jock said, "I'm burstin' for a pish."

Euan and Stuart stood by a bin finishing their chips and watched Ian and Jock walk on ahead.

"I have to say Euan," Stuart said, "I wasn't expecting this tonight."

"I wonder if he does this every Friday night?"

"No fucking idea. He told me he was looking for someone. Didn't get much more out of him though, I don't think he likes me much."

"No, me neither," Euan laughed.

"I think it's just his way," Stuart tried to reassure him. "Told him about my Dad and stuff but he seemed quite dismissive. I was pouring my heart out to the old git too."

"Seems to like Ian though."

"Aye, 'cos he's a big ginger nationalist, that's why. I'm with you on this one Euan - can't really see the point of changing things for the sake of it. We all hate the fucking Tories, but they get their few years in the sun, then it'll be Labour's turn again. Swings and roundabouts. Anyway, this time next year I'll be lying on my patio with a big fucking gin and tonic, so I really couldn't give a damn."

Euan pondered this for a moment and said, "Lucky bastard. So the house is nearly finished?"

"Pretty much. Ten years of hard graft but I've just about got it to a state I'd be happy to live in. I'm going back over in a couple of weeks to do a bit more. It was practically a ruin when I bought it remember?"

Euan did remember. Stuart was embarking on his French

adventure just as he was setting out on his disastrous life with Vicki. In ten years, Stuart had built a home while Euan's had crumbled around him.

"Yeah you've done alright Stuart. I've been following your progress on Facebook, the place looks amazing." He stopped and nodded towards Ian and Jock, "What's he up to now?"

They looked to see Jock and Ian stand against an old blue police box. One of the few that hadn't yet been converted into a coffee booth. Ian was laughing and shaking his head at Jock, but the old man kept grabbing Ian and positioning him directly in front of him.

Jock turned to face the box, where there was a large poster advertising a forthcoming exhibition at the National Museum - the work of William Murdoch, a Scottish Inventor.

They watched as Jock took the rubber stopper off the bottom of his aluminium walking stick and another from the end of the curved part of the handle.

"What the fuck is he doing?" asked Stuart.

"I imagine we're about to find out, I'm staying over here though."

Jock stood still, as if he was studying the poster and seemed to be positioning the curved part of the walking stick into the front of his trousers, while pointed the long end behind him, towards the gutter.

Ian was struggling to contain his laughter now, as he turned his back to Jock to face the street.

A stream of urine rolled quietly out of the end of the stick and towards a drain in the gutter.

"He's having some sort of covert, undercover pish by the looks of things," Euan said.

A policeman walked past, oblivious to the crime that was being committed under his nose.

"The man's a genius."

CHAPTER EIGHT

Rosie

Rosie arrived at Deacon Brodie's to find the place buzzing with chatter. She made her way to the bar past several animated conversations.

"...Ran a knife right over his throat."

"...A straw, a fucking straw!"

"...Bunch of fucking neds."

"...He was a fat bastard, choked on his bubble gum apparently."

"...Is it not a trachybottomy?"

"...Aye, the mother was on Jeremy Kyle once."

"...Got taken away in an ambulance."

Oh no, she thought, Jock? Was he okay? She got to the bar and leaned over. "Excuse me!"

"Just a minute," the barmaid said; she was busy typing on her phone. She slowly wandered up the bar, looking at her phone all the time, then stopped typing. Looked at the screen for a minute and said, "Yes, sorry, had something I had to Tweet there, what can I get you?"

"I'm looking for an old man, ninety-five years old, red tartan trousers. Here's a picture of him from about..."

"I don't need to see the picture, yes he was here. He's a hero, is he your grandad or something?"

"Erm, no, but I do look after him. He's from the care home I work at, and I'm just trying to get his medication to him. How do you mean a hero?"

The barmaid recounted Jock's life-saving operation on the recently acquitted Bubbles.

"Oh my god!" Rosie laughed. "He did that? Really? Did he seem okay? Who was he with?"

"Three guys, late thirties, maybe forty. Hard to tell. One of them looked about sixty but that was probably just his beard. He was fine. He left here a hero, honestly. Seemed quite chipper."

Rosie could barely contain her relief. "Thanks, I've been chasing him for hours. Any idea where they were headed?"

"No sorry, they left about half an hour ago, maybe less. There's tons of pubs around here though, they could be anywhere."

Oh crap, thought Rosie. The barmaid was right. Deacon Brodie's sat on a crossroads. The Lawnmarket led back to the castle, the Mound wound its way down towards Princes Street, George IV bridge, which she'd sped up earlier, led back to the Meadows, and that left the High Street. Which was still mobbed with tourists.

Which way now? She needed to think, she'd check the pubs in the area on her phone, look for ones he'd be likely to go to. She took a barstool and ordered a coke.

"Just a coke?" asked the barmaid.

"Yes," then, "No, can I have some crisps too please. Cheese and onion."

"No problem," the barmaid filled a coke glass from the pump. "I'm sure he'll be fine," she said, "Don't worry about it." She place the coke and crisps on the bar.

It sounds like he's okay, she thought as she sipped the coke through a straw. The guys he's with will take care of him. And hopefully they'll get him back to the home safe and sound. But what if they're not what they seem? They might abduct him, batter him, leave him dead in an alleyway? Oh god. Surely not. That little bald guy wasn't the type. And the one with the beard looked nice enough. Appearances can be deceptive though. They could be murderers. Jesus Rosie, calm yourself down.

She was thumbing through lists of Edinburgh pubs, there were bloody loads of them, he could be anywhere now, when her phone rang.

"Hello, Sheila... no, I'm eating crisps... he hasn't?... no, well he's been quite busy by the sound of things! I think he's okay though, he's with a group of blokes apparently... sounds like they're on a pub crawl... ... ... he said what? Well tell Mr Urquhart that I'm trying to do him a bloody favour, the ungrateful sod... ... ... no, I won't leave it! Jock's still out here, somewhere and until he's taken his bloody tablets I'm not giving up... ... okay Sheila, will do.... Yeah, call me if he shows up... Bye."

She drained the last of her coke and headed out the door.

Rosie looked down the hill where it turned past the Bank of Scotland's headquarters. This road curved down from the high ridge of the High Street down into the New Town, where the pubs were pricier and had a younger crowd. George IV Bridge headed back towards the Meadows, and was a possibility. She racked her brains, thinking about the types of pubs he'd be likely to go to. There was Greyfriars Bobby, or a couple on Victoria Street, which got her thinking about all the pubs on the Grassmarket beyond and her head began to swim.

No, she thought, he'd keep going down the High Street, she was sure of it. She looked down towards the mass of St Giles cathedral and the mobs of tourists cramming the streets. Plenty people to ask anyway. She crossed the road and passed a large statue of a seated man with an outstretched toe. She'd always wondered why his toe was shiny brass but the rest of him was green.

Beyond him, a golden mime stood on a small box. Charlie Chaplin. Still as a statue. A small crowd stood and stared, and took photographs.

She heard a tourist say, "He's still here, he's been standing there all day. That can't be good for you."

All day, she thought. She approached Charlie Chaplin and said, "Excuse me, I'm looking for a ninety-five year old man. I think he was with three other men. Have you seen him pass here today?"

The mime stared straight ahead.

"Look, he's very vulnerable. He needs medication. I need to find him."

The mime kept staring, although his eyes seemed to narrow slightly.

Rosie stared at him, "Hello? Mr Chaplin? Can you hear me?"

She heard a long breath being expelled from Charlie's nostrils, he gave a barely noticeable nod.

"Good, did you see him?"

Another nod, and a twitch of the moustache.

"Which way did he go?"

Charlie nodded his head to the left, indicating the High Street.

"Thanks," said Rosie. "Did you hear them talking? Any indication of where they were headed?"

Charlie whispered, through gritted teeth, "No. Look, fuck off will you, I'm meant to be a fucking statue."

Rosie looked through the crowds of tourists mobbing the High Street. He was down there somewhere, she thought, so she started walking, asking passers-by if they'd seen an old man in red tartan trousers. Most shook their heads, they'd been watching fire-eaters, or jugglers, or acrobats. None had seen an old man in regimental dress. She tried the newsagents, and the restaurants. She tried St Giles cathedral and Parliament Square. Nothing. There were a couple of pubs on this stretch, but she drew a blank there too.

She stood in the middle of the High Street, looking up and down for a glimpse of him in the crowds. She caught a glimpse of red tartan and looked, but it was a couple of teenage girls, one wearing a tartan jacket. As they passed, she overheard a snippet of their conversation. "He was ancient, it was so funny. Stood up on the Mercat Cross giving it this totally random speech."

"Excuse me, sorry, who was doing that?" she interrupted and explained her reasons.

"Just this random old guy, stood up there making a big speech to the crowd. I filmed it on my phone, look."

She showed Rosie the clip. It was Jock! What the hell was he up to?

"When was this?" asked Rosie.

The girl looked to her friend, "Dunno, what, about half an hour ago?" Her friend nodded in agreement.

"Did you see where he went?"

"No, sorry, kept going down the High Street I think, we were heading the other way."

She pressed on, it was half-past eight now. An hour and a half and she'd phone the police, if he hadn't shown up back at the home. She tried a few more restaurants and shops, with no luck, then saw a police box. Aha, my sentinels, she thought as she stepped up the pace, but this was one of the few that hadn't been turned into a coffee hut. Perhaps because it was positioned immediately outside an American coffee shop. She stood there, looking around. It stank a bit of piss around here she thought. Must have been the tramps on Hunter Square, pissing against the police box. She looked down and saw a trail of urine leading down the drain. Oddly, it seemed to start just before the drain. Must've been a kid. She remembered being held over a gutter once in York while her mum pulled her trousers down and let her pee directly down the drain. God, what an embarrassment, she thought. Then realised she needed another pee herself.

There were public loos on Hunter Square, but she hated using them. They stank, so she nipped into the coffee shop and used the facilities there. The place was full of well-dressed young tourists, chatting and sipping over-priced coffees. You could do this anywhere in the world, she thought. You're in the centre of one of the most beautiful cities on Earth and you're sitting in the same bloody coffee shop you've probably got in your own town. She didn't understand the appeal. She'd have sought out a local place, with a bit of character, and left with the satisfaction that the money she'd spent would probably be spent somewhere else locally, keeping everyone happy, and everyone in business. Not disappearing into an off-shore bank account for tax-evasion purposes. Did people even care these days? She didn't think so.

This allowed her to leave without spending any money, and free from guilt. Although she did feel bad about nicking a bundle of hand-towels from the toilet.

Okay, couple of pubs down here she thought and headed into Blair Street.

The first was a sprawling place, over two floors. It was full of students and tourists and after a long wait, she left with the knowledge that he hadn't been seen in there.

She looked across the road The City Cafe. A cafe? Would he go there? Might have fancied a cuppa she supposed so walked past the bouncers with a smile. Why would you need bouncers for a cafe? She thought.

A minute later she was back on the street. That was certainly not the kind of place Jock would have gone. Although his trousers may have gone down a storm with the patrons.

She continued down towards the Cowgate, looking left and right at the junction. Plenty of pubs down here, but again, mostly student crowds. She turned and headed back up to Hunter Square.

Her phone rang. She checked the screen. 'Fraser Urquhart'.

"Hello Fraser... yes I'm still looking for him... no I haven't told the police... well he seems to be causing quite a stir, let's put it that way... well, where do I start? He's gifted an antique book to a homeless man, donated some medals to his regimental museum at the castle, performed an emergency operation on a recently acquitted thug and made a stirring speech for Scottish independence in front of a crowd of hundreds... I don't know if he mentioned Urquhart House in any of this, no. Frankly, I doubt it... Yes, well if he hasn't shown up in an hour, I'm calling them... I don't care Fraser... I'm calling the police in one hour, and you should show a bit of gratitude here, I'm trying to do you a favour... ... ... You'd sack me for what? Fraser, if he suffers as a result of missing his medication, it's going to make the papers anyway... because I'll tell them how you refused to involve the police earlier, that's how... Your reputation won't be so bloody glorious then will it?"

She hung up. What an absolute dickhead! She was shaking. Fraser had threatened her with the sack. How could she go back there now? She needed a new job. There was no way she could work for this man anymore. Plenty of agency work out there for a qualified geriatric nurse. She'd miss Jock terribly though, and Sheila - they'd been friends for years. Christ, this was all she needed. Right, focus Rosie. Jock. Tablets. Get him back to the home and get home to your bed. Register with an agency tomorrow and she could be out of there in a month.

CHAPTER NINE

The Mitre

They crossed the busy junction with North Bridge without incident as, by chance more than anything, the pedestrian crossing showed a green man. Not that Jock had even looked at it before raising his stick and stepping onto the road. Leaving the jugglers and fire-eaters behind they carried on to the next stretch of the High Street.

Jock was explaining something to Ian, "...aye, pneumatic tubes. The messages got fired aboot the offices and shops in an instant."

"And I bet none of them had ads for Viagra in them?" joked Ian.

"I've nae idea what ye're on aboot son."

"That was a neat move back there Jock," said Euan, pointing his thumb back towards the police box.

"Och aye, well - necessity is the mother of invention, as they say. I cut the top off the handle and stuck another stopper on it, gives me a hollow tube, and allows me tae pish intae my bedpan without getting oot my bed."

Ian looked at the walking stick, a sticker on the side said:

'Property: Urquhart House.'

"Is that your care home, Urquhart House? Should we not let them know you're okay?"

"No need for that son, I'll be hame soon. Come on, I've got a mouth like sandpaper, this'll do."

They looked up at the pub sign, 'The Mitre, Wine and Spirit Merchant.' It was just after 8pm, and the sun was gone. The High Street was bathed in the bluish glow of dusk.

There was a decent crowd in, a mix of tourists and locals, and a generally happy atmosphere in The Mitre.

Stuart and Euan headed for the bar while Ian and Jock managed to grab a table by the window, underneath a towering bookcase.

Euan's phone chirped. Another text message from Vicki: "Change of plan. I'm staying at D's for rest of weekend. Call me. V."

He stopped in his tracks, "Get the drinks in Stuart, I need to make a call." He turned and headed back out of the door where he stood for a moment, looking at the message again. 'Call me'. That was ominous. What was so important it couldn't go in a text message?

Outside, there were a few tables with tourists and locals enjoying a cigarette. He stepped past the bouncer and walked towards the edge of the pavement then, with a deep breath, called Vicki, his heart pounding - his mouth drying up. The ringtone seemed louder than usual. More threatening, if that were possible. She answered.

"Hi, it's me, don't know why this can't wait - you're enjoying yourself, and for once I'm having a good fucking time too, so what's so important?.... ...."

In an instant, with two words, Euan's world was turned on its head. He put his hand to his forehead and started walking, looking for something to lean on. An overflowing litter bin offered him some support. Vicki was still talking, but, through her tears, he could barely make out a word she was saying.

He gathered his senses and suddenly the world seemed clearer, brighter, and more full of promise than he could ever have imagined. He cut in, his voice calm, "Vicki, I'm happy for you... ... I am, really... no I don't care... ... ... okay, Christ, of course I care, you know what I mean... We've both known this was coming... no, no really, I'll be fine. Go. Let's not make this any harder. We'll talk tomorrow. Don't worry about me. Luckily, I'm already pished, otherwise I might have taken the news a bit less gracefully, but you know, I'm out with my mates, I'm having a good time. You're obviously having a good time... ... ... spare me the details... ... ... look, just fucking go will you."

He hung up. His head was buzzing, tourists swarmed past him, oblivious to the life-changing event that he'd just experienced. He stared back up the Royal Mile, and the castle where their pub crawl had begun just a few hours ago. What a difference a few pints and the odd whisky can make, he thought.

He became aware of a dampness on his backside and quickly stepped away from the litter bin he'd been leaning on. He touched the wet, warm patch on his jeans and nervously brought his hand back around, it was covered in thick brown liquid. Oh shit, he thought and sniffed carefully. He'd never been so happy to smell brown chip-shop sauce in his life, and burst out laughing.

As he stepped back into The Mitre Vicki's words - "It's over" - unspoken for so long, were spinning around his head. Ten years passed in an instant before his eyes. He approached Stuart and leant on the bar, dizzy with the enormity of the situation, but instead of sadness, he felt relief. Elation almost, as the burden of the years of guilt - for the abortion, and for their miserable life together - was lifted from his shoulders. "It's over, it's over," he started singing an old REM song to himself.

"Everything okay?" Stuart asked.

"Everything's fucking fine!" said Euan, looking around the

pub with what seemed like colour vision, after years of living in black and white. "Vicki's left me."

"Eh? Fucking hell. You're grinning all over your fucking face. Does this call for a celebration?"

"I think so," said Euan, "Get a bottle of something, here." He handed Stuart a £50 note and went to tell Ian and Jock his news.

Stuart joined them a few minutes later with three pints and another malt for Jock. "The barmaid's bringing the rest over."

Ian patted Euan on the shoulder. "Maybe it's for the best eh? Look I'll be honest with you, 'cause I feel I can be now. Nobody liked her anyway."

Euan laughed and said, "I'm not sure I did either."

He looked around the table. Ian, his best mate in the world, seemed genuinely happy for him. How many years had he been keeping quiet about his opinion of Vicki? What a fucking mug he'd been all these years. Everyone must have been ripping the piss out of him behind his back. Stuart was his usual indifferent self, but what did he know about relationships? He'd never been with anyone for more than a fucking week. Then he turned to Jock, who was smiling at him with those twinkling eyes. Jock raised his whisky towards Euan and started singing that song again, "Oh why should I be so sad on my wedding day?"

The barmaid arrived with a tray and set out four fluted glasses on the table.

"Here you go, enjoy!" she said as she placed a bottle of champagne on the table.

"Champagne?" Euan looked at Stuart, his eyes questioning the choice.

"Well you said get a bottle, and it's a celebration," Stuart said.

"As long as it's wet, it'll do me," said Jock, pouring it wildly into the glasses, the foam frothing up and spilling all over the table.

"Booze is booze," laughed Ian. He raised his glass, "To Euan, lang may yer lum reek, and soon may you get your hole!"

"Cheers!" they shouted together.

Twenty minutes of Euan's animated babble followed. Ian could tell this may have been the best thing that had happened to his old friend in a long time. Where did the years go? It was so easy to get stuck in a rut. His eyes were drawn to a TV showing footage of a rapidly billowing smoke cloud.

"Hard to believe that was thirteen years ago," Ian said, nodding towards the TV.

"Fuck aye, September 11th, right enough," said Euan.

"And what followed?" said Ian, looking at Euan. "A fucking illegal war that cost hundreds of thousands of lives and billions of pounds. And for what? Fucking oil. Fucking US corporations. Fuck all to do with the terrorist attack. Wrong country for a start."

"Aye, I know," said Euan, "I was on that march too remember?"

Ian remembered the "Don't Attack Iraq" march in Glasgow. They'd all gone through for it. Millions had marched across the world. But the UK and USA had gone ahead with their immoral and illegal war anyway.

"That was your fucking glorious Labour party Euan, remember that when you're voting no next week in the hope they'll get their eight years in the sun soon."

Euan sighed, "Aye, well - better than the Tories eh?"

"Are they?" said Ian. "Really? How? Where's the difference in their policies? They want to privatise everything too. More cuts, more austerity. All for the good of the City of London. And what about Clause 4? You can't just remove a cornerstone of your party's constitution and claim to be the same party."

Euan dismissed this with a wave of the hand. He had no idea what Ian was talking about. "So we vote Yes next week and what? We get rid of Trident? How does that make us safer?"

"What fucking use is a nuclear missile against terrorists Euan? What are you going to do with them? Drop a nuke on a bus with a suspected rucksack bomber on it? There's no fucking conventional threat anymore. We'll save hundreds of millions. And they can fucking take them with them. You know they're sitting 20 miles outside our biggest city because they said they were 'too dangerous' to be housed anywhere in England? Are you not starting to see the real reasons behind Better fucking Together yet?"

Euan laughed and shook his head, "Hey don't harsh my buzz man. This might be the best night of my life, can we change the subject?"

Ian sat back and laughed, "Aye okay. Just fucking… THINK before you vote eh? Please?" He paused and took a large mouthful of beer. Euan had had enough. Time to ease off for a bit. "So, Jock - these medals of yours, what's the story?"

Jock looked every day of his ninety-five years now. He'd been quiet, just letting the lads do the talking, and Ian thought he'd better get him back into the conversation before he fell asleep.

"Eh? Oh, aye, there were three medals worthy o' a story I suppose. Where do I begin?" Jock began. He took another mouthful of whisky, swirled it around his mouth and grimaced as it hit his stomach.

"You alright there?" asked Ian.

"Fine son, aye. Right, Military Medal. For Bravery in the Field. 1942. We'd charged oor tanks at the Germans. Like I said, we were a mounted division, and this carried through tae the way we attacked. We caught the buggers napping. I fired off aboot ten shells, I was the gunner ye see, before oor tank was hit by artillery. The tracks were buckled, so we jumped oot. Two of the boys got fried by machine gun fire, but I carried on wi' nothing but my Sten gun, and these things were shite. Jammed all the time. And in the desert, wi' all that sand, they were even worse. Well, I came around a sand dune and found mysel' looking at aboot twenty Germans, who were running aboot daft, loading shells into their artillery guns. I opened up on them, but nothing happened. The Sten was jammed. I thought to myself - 'Shite Jock, you've got yersel' into a right scrape here,' and tried tae sneak away, but just as I did one of oor tanks came crashing over the ridge o' the dune. The Germans fell back, reaching for grenades, and firing off their machine guns, which of course, are nae use against a tank. Two more of oor boys came battering over the ridge, and the Germans looked like they'd had enough. So I stood there, pointed my gun at them, which wisnae working, and shouted 'Hande Hoch'. Well, the buggers shat themselves, and stuck their hands in the air. Their officer barked the order tae surrender, and that was that, we'd taken eleven artillery guns and about three hundred German prisoners."

"Holy crap!" said Ian, mouth open.

"That's mental," said Euan.

"Now if ye get me another drink I'll tell ye about my Distinguished Conduct Medal, that's for real bravery."

Ian got the round in, returning with four pints this time. "Thought you could do with a wee break from the whisky Jock so I got you an Edinburgh Gold, it's a nice ale, local, you'll like it."

"Ach, I'll be pishin' it oot in no time, thanks though son."

Jock was just about to start his next story when Stuart ducked and said, "Oh shit!"

"What?" asked Euan.

"It's the woman from the train I was telling you about, the chubby gobshite - she's just walked in."

Euan turned to see a large woman in a flowery dress stagger towards the bar on high heels. Her friend was helping to keep her upright by the looks of it.

"She looks like fun," said Euan.

"That must be her sister, said she was up to meet her." Stuart sank into his chair and shielded his face with his hand. "Anyway, come on Jock, next medal..."

"Right, aye, Distinguished Conduct Medal. Speaks for itself. 1942."

They all leaned forward.

"A month later we found ourselves in another scrap. We had fifteen tanks, Shermans and Stuarts, that's what I was in. They were falling tae bits, and Stuarts were funny things - had a side-mounted gun that had plenty up-and-down movement, but no' much side-to-side. You were relying on the driver pointing ye in the right direction most o' the time. Anyway, we'd hammered into this village and took another couple o' hundred German prisoners, when we saw a dust-cloud approaching. We jumped back into the tanks and counted thirty panzers belting towards us. We were outnumbered two tae one, and boy did we gie them a battle. Terrifying it was, but we held our positions and my driver, cannae remember his name, got us intae this alleyway. Well, he didnae see the German tank approaching from the side. It took a pop at us, but missed and blew up a hoose and we ended up tipping sideways into the cellar. The boy must've thought he'd killed us, so he trundled on. So there we are, in a tank on its side, down a hole, and I wis struggling tae work out what way was up when I heard the clatter of a wall falling down outside. I looked oot the hatch and saw two panzers, just sittin' there. They must have been considering their next move, but I realised that, as we were lying on our side, that by aimin' the gun high I could point the thing right at the bastards! So I loaded up a 75mm shell and boom! Took one of them out, the ammo exploded inside and up it went. The other one tried tae move out the road, but he was trapped, so I fired off another shell and bingo. Two panzers up in smoke, from a tank that wisnae even the right way up!"

This was even more interesting than debugging bank

computer software, Euan thought to himself.

Ian was just stunned. His life - with his safe job, his wife, his kids, and all that security - seemed undeserved, unearned. How could a man go through all this and end up living in a home? There should be a 5-star hotel somewhere for war veterans to spend their last days, paid for by the state. Instead we were bailing out the criminal weasels who gambled with our money and brought the world to its knees, while they laughed at us and sailed the world in luxury liners. This wouldn't happen in an independent Scotland, he thought. Those fuckers would be first against the wall. Iceland had the right idea, jail the bankers, help the poor. Another small country that was doing just fine.

"Jock, I can't believe this. Why aren't you famous? There should be a statue of you out on that High Street for fuck's sake."

Jock just said, "I was one o' many son. Just doin' my job. Whose round is it?"

They were losing track now, the booze was wrapping the world in a glow of camaraderie, mild confusion and that overwhelming sense of love you feel for your fellow man. Stuart in particular seemed to be feeling it as he had left the table to chat to a bloke that had been hanging around their table, eavesdropping on Jock's story as he became more and more animated.

"I'll get them, what'll it be?" said Ian.

"I'll go back on the whisky son, I'll need tae go for a pish now. Don't get me another pint." Jock stood up and swayed, then sat back down again with a bump.

"Are you alright?" asked Euan.

"Aye," said Jock. Just stood up too quick there, I'm oot o' breath wi' all this story telling."

"Get me a JD and coke," said Euan. I'm off the malt now I think." He had that dopey grin that always meant it was time to start on the alternative drinks, safe in the drunken knowledge that a change was as good as a rest.

"Rock and roll," said Ian. He tapped Stuart on the shoulder, interrupting his conversation with the eavesdropper. "Drink?"

Stuart had the look too, wide-eyed and sleepy looking. "I'll have another whisky, whatever, a pint, or something. What are you having?" he staggered slightly.

"Dunno," said Ian, "an Edinburgh Gold maybe, aye, fancy one of them?"

"I do," Stuart said, "I do, aye. One of them then."

As Ian edged his way to the bar he heard a scream of "Hello handsome!" - it was the woman Stuart had met on the train, she'd finally spotted him. Although he had abandoned his cover somewhat. As she bumped her way through the crowd towards him his face changed from happy drunk to terrified rabbit.

"I just knew I'd bump into you!" Sharon screamed as she gave Stuart a lung threatening hug. "This is my sister," she turned and shouted back towards the bar, "Emily! Come here, this is the male model I was telling you about!"

Stuart looked like he wished a hole would open up like the one Jock's tank had fallen into. He was doing his best to be polite, but it wasn't really necessary as Sharon was doing all the talking. Her sister had joined them now, and they were like two very large peas in a very large pod.

Ian edged past with the drinks, handing Stuart his pint in passing. Sharon looked him up and down and said, "Oh who's Mr Beardy then?"

Stuart, although drunk, had enough wits about him to seize the opportunity. "This is my good mate Ian, a nicer man you couldn't hope to meet. Ian, Sharon, Sharon, Ian." He grabbed Ian as he placed the drinks on the table and spun him around.

"Hello, erm, Sharon," said Ian, "So, you met Stuart on the train?"

"He's been telling you?!" she waggled Stuart's cheek, "I knew I made an impact on him!"

Stuart grimaced and turned back to his friend, subtly edging him away a few feet.

Euan and Jock clinked glasses and watched the events unfold with amusement.

"So son, you're still all for the union then?" asked Jock.

Euan sighed, "I guess so. Look Jock, I work for a bank. I know we're the 'bad guys' but I honestly think that there's no point closing ourselves off. We work okay as a bigger unit; as far as I can see, we've got more clout. A problem shared is a problem halved and all that. And given the mess the economy's in, we should be grateful of their help. I can't see us affording the bank bailouts on our own."

"That's shite son, if ye don't mind me sayin'" said Jock, "I might be an auld man but I can read, and I can see through the lies that we're fed. We'd have had nae mare share o' the bailout tae pay if we'd been independent. And I'll tell ye this, if we had been independent, we'd never have let it get intae that state in the first place. It's the gung-ho attitude o' the gamblers down south that caused it. Like I telt ye - nothin' good can come o' gamblin'. It's those bastards that should be payin' tae fix this country, no the pensioners, or the workers."

Euan took a long gulp of his pint. These bloody nationalists were full of facts weren't they? What was wrong with just going on your gut instinct? "Maybe Jock, but here's the thing. I like the English!"

"So do I," said Jock. "It's got nothing tae do wi' hating the English ye know. In fact, I think a lot o' them would be happier without us. If they held the referendum down there it'd be interestin' tae see the result. They didnae want the union in 1707 either, almost as much as we didnae. I reckon they'd be pleased tae set us adrift, based on the rubbish they're fed about us lot bein' a burden on them. But I also reckon some o' the smart ones would probably move up here; they're as sick o' the shite that passes for politics in Westminster these days as we are. And I'm all for that. Ye need a good mix o' cultures and nationalities tae make a nation. Don't think this is all about jingoistic nationalism. I've been a Labour voter all my life."

"Me too," said Euan.

Jock sat back and took another drink of his whisky. He stopped and held onto the table's edge.

"Jock?" Euan leaned forward, "...Jock, are you okay?"

Jock looked at Euan like he'd never seen him before, staring out - the twinkle in his eyes dulled for a moment. He coughed and took a deep breath, "I'm fine son. It's the whisky, gies me heartburn."

"...Jenners, lovely place, have you been? Of course you've been. And we were at Harvey Nic's, the restaurant at the top, lovely views, have you been there? The sushi is to die for!" Sharon barely paused for breath.

"No," said Ian, desperate to escape the tedious stream of shite that was pouring from Sharon's sizeable mouth. "I've got a thing about paying a fortune for a meal that wouldn't feed one of my kids. And to be honest, I couldn't care less what way it's arranged on the plate. You know what I like most in the world? Stovies. Stovies and brown sauce. And my kids love it too. We're simple folk up here you know..." That should do it, he thought.

"Oh you've got kids?" Sharon said, unable to contain her disappointment. "Well, I thought it was very reasonable. Food was lovely. So, who's your friend there?" she looked down at Euan.

"This, Sharon, is Euan. He's loaded. And single."

Euan looked up in horror as Ian smiled the daftest smile he could manage and gave him two thumbs up before disappearing to the toilet.

When he returned, they were all sitting down around the table. Stuart's friend had left, and he was staring absently at his mobile phone. Jock was laughing with Sharon's sister Emily, and Euan was doing his best to edge his seat as far from Sharon as he could, who responded by shuffling her chair even closer. It was like one of Jock's tank battles.

Ian sat down, it was dark outside now. They should probably think about getting Jock home, they'd met him just after five, and he'd no idea how long he'd been in The Ensign Ewart before they arrived. He'd had a skinful, couldn't be good for him, at that age. But first, he had another medal story to tell.

"So Jock, you said you had three medals worthy of a story?"

Jock's chest swelled as he made himself as big as he could. He had the attention of the table now. "That I did, aye. The Victoria Cross. For Valour. June 1944."

Given the previous stories, Ian wasn't sure how he could possibly have topped them. Bravery, distinguished conduct, and now valour? He supped his pint expectantly.

"It was a few days after the Normandy landings, me and the boy Goolies were sent out on patrol in oor new Sherman tank, much better than they other bloody things. Had a proper gun, for a start. So, we were trundlin' along this wee country road, no' far from where we were camped. The sergeant just wanted us tae take a look at the next village - we'd heard there was a German unit holed up there. We were just to get within binocular distance and report back. Well, the thing was, we were both fucking steaming. We'd uncovered a wine cellar in a bombed-out house the night before - we'd been up all night drinking, and Goolies took us down the wrong road."

"Hang on," said Euan, "steaming? In charge of a tank?"

"Listen son, if you'd been through what we'd been through you'd have been steaming tae. Those beaches were hell, utter hell."

"We've seen Saving Private Ryan," said Emily.

"Aye well, it was much worse than that hen. Anyway, we're trundlin' along this road and Goolies is all over the place, running intae the hedges, knocking down telegraph poles, and I was laughin' and had just said 'for fucksake Goolies, straighten it up man' when the world went arse-about-tit and we ended up lying on our side in a ditch at the side of the road."

"Again?" laughed Ian.

"Aye son, it was becomin' a habit." Jock laughed and took a drink. "So, I managed tae stand up, on the inside wall and shouted tae Goolies that we had tae get oot, but there was nae response. I looked through tae the driver's seat and saw him, slumped tae one side, and covered in blood. His head was split open. The daft bastard wisnae wearing his helmet and had cracked his skull like a walnut on the side of the tank. These things weren't exactly built for comfort ye know?"

"Jesus," Stuart said, eyes dancing. He was struggling to focus now.

"So, I'm checkin' his neck for a pulse, but there's nothin', when I felt the ground start tae shake. A wee rumble at first, but when I heard the rattle of tank tracks I feared the worst. I slid open the observation hatch, and just aboot shat myself. There was a German tank coming doon the road towards us. One of the new ones, I thought, must be a Panther. I hadn't seen one yet, but I'd heard all aboot them. Armour was much thicker than the rest, and it had a fuckin' huge gun that was slowly turning tae face me. Well, I've never moved so fast in my life, and it's no' easy operatin' a gun in a tank that's lying sideyways, especially when you're half-cut. But I was in luck, my gun wis aimin' just aboot directly at the bugger, so I cranked it a wee bit, got the Panther in my sights and fired off a 75mm shell. Kaboom!"

"You got it?" asked Ian.

"Eventually, " said Jock. "But my shell just skited right off the bloody thing. There was a shower o' sparks and I saw the shell disappear over a hedgerow. I thought tae myself 'This is it Jock'. I'd just met Ellie, a few weeks before the landings, and she was all I could think aboot. I just kept her face in my mind as I waited tae die. The Panther had stopped. I could see right down the barrel o' its gun. A perfect black circle. All I could hear was the sound of a train approaching the village, when BOOM!" he threw his hands in the air.

"It hit you?" asked Euan.

"No, there was a huge explosion fae over the hedge, and the Panther was hit by a dozen shells at once. He must've thought he'd been outflanked. I saw the turret spin round quickly and fire off intae the hedge, BANG! Then there was an almighty racket as all hell broke loose."

"It hadn't already?" said Euan.

"The Panther was on fire now, and I saw three boys jump out the hatch, in flames. They didnae last long. The air was filled with the sound of stuff crashing down, ear-splitting it was. Behind the burnt-out tank I saw a huge cloud o' dust go up in the village. Then silence."

Five mouths hung open around the table. Even Sharon was listening.

"I popped open the hatch and crawled oot, grabbing my rifle. Now, I was drunk, but some things sober ye up quite quickly and what I saw certainly did that. I edged forwards towards the Panther, black smoke belching oot o' the thing. The boys that had escaped were lying on the grass verge, like three burnt sausages. I didnae know how many crew these things had, but anybody still inside would've been dead as well, so I peeked over the hedge to see who'd taken the shots at the Panther, expecting to see a few of our tanks at least, but all that was there was a burning truck. And a German truck at that. From the occasional bangs coming from the flames, I guessed it was an ammo truck. And it was sittin' right about where my shell had gone after it bounced off the Panther. So, aye, that'd been a lucky shot right enough. The ammo truck had blown up and peppered the Panther with German shells."

"That was lucky," said Euan, looking around the table at the awestruck group.

"What about the dust cloud in the village?" Ian asked.

"I'm comin' tae that."

There was a noise from outside, laughter, a group of the lads from Deacon Brodie's, Bubbles' mates. They were trying to get in but the bouncer was having none of it. "It's full boys, sorry."

Jock glanced at them then continued, "So, I'm makin' my way towards the village. Beautiful day it was, and all I could hear was a wood pigeon coo-ing in a tree. I was thinking of Ellie, and how picturin' her face had been the thing that'd saved me. She was looking oot for me. I was sure of it. There was still this big cloud o' dust hangin' over the village as I edged past the first house. I turned a corner and saw where it was coming fae."

"Come on man, just let us in for fuck's sake!" one of the crowd was arguing with the bouncer now.

They all glanced around, but were too lost in Jock's story, so turned back and urged him to continue.

"There was a big black supply train, in the middle of the street. Must've been the one I'd heard from the tank. It'd ploughed through three hooses. There was a huge hole in the side of the engine. I had a look and thought it looked like a shell had hit it. Then it struck me, the shell the Panther had fired off intae the hedge must've hit the train and derailed it. Christ, I thought, that shell I fired was a lucky shot like nae other!"

"Holy shit," said Ian, "so you took out a tank, an ammo truck and a train with one shot?"

"There's more than that," Jock said, taking another drink of his whisky.

The bouncer had stood his ground and Bubbles' mates had taken the hint. They marched off down the High Street shouting abuse back at him. All was quiet again, apart from the babble of pub chatter.

"So, the train driver was dead, as was the engineer. They'd been smashed against the engine as it hit the hooses. The rest o' the train was just cargo, supply carriages. Full o' ammo and rations. I crawled under the engine and stopped as I heard

German voices, but I soon realised it was coming fae a radio. Frantic stuff. All one-way, the same phrase, repeated. I edged forward under the train, on my elbows. A load o' paper blew across the road in front o' me, and I could still hear this radio, crackling away. The same phrase, lookin' for an answer, but getting nae response. I crawled out fae under the train, stood up, and looked intae the ruins of the house. And ye'd never believe it - the train had steamed right intae what looked like the headquarters o' a German unit. The radio set lay on its back, but that was the only thing makin' a noise. It was full o' bodies. A terrible sight. Some crushed by the train, the rest killed by the hoose fallin' doon on top o' them."

They could only shake their heads in admiration. This was unbelievable, thought Ian. A single shell, and he takes out a tank, an ammo truck, a supply train and a whole German unit. While pished. And the shell didn't even damage the original target!

"And that's how I got the Victoria Cross," Jock sat back, blue eyes twinkling.

They raised their glasses and Ian shouted, "To Jock, war hero and pisshead. And here's tae us! Wha's like us?"

"Damn few, and they're a' deid!" finished Euan.

Sharon burst out laughing, leaning into Euan and brushing his arm with her sizeable chest. "You're funny!" She stroked his bald head.

Stuart was fading fast now. "I'm fucking pished," he said to Ian. "Not sure I'll manage many more. Might have to head home soon."

"Ach come on, we'll not see you again for five years probably. Man up! Get yourself a coke or something."

Stuart nodded, "Good idea." He rose, and staggered his way to the bar.

"Right Jock," said Ian, "can I just say that you have made this evening for us? I am so glad we bumped into you. You're an inspiration. A hero. A fucking fine man. Definitely the finest ninety-five year old I've ever met. But I think we need to be getting you home now. Want me to call you a cab?" Ian asked. He didn't have long now to work on converting Euan to his cause, and Jock looked like he really needed his bed.

"No laddie! I'm fine, I'll have another couple, then I'll head. There's a pub down the road I want tae show you. I'm lookin' for somebody mind, I hope I might find him there."

"Well, okay, if you're sure. Want us to phone the home, let them know you're okay?"

"No, there's no need. I'm fine son, don't worry. I'll be home soon enough."

Ian thought about it; no harm in letting them know. "I'm just going for a pish."

At the back of the pub Ian got out his phone and called home, "Hi love, it's me... Aye I'm pished. How are the kids? ... Aww, bless... Aye I know, I'll buy it tomorrow, the party's on Sunday. How's you? ... Good. Feet up then. And no drinking! Listen, could you do me a favour, long story, I'll tell you tomorrow, but could you look up the number for Urquhart House care home and text me it... No I'm not putting you in a home... Me? Aye I could probably do with it. I know... Right, got to dash. Stuart's blootered and Euan's wife's left him. I'll tell you all about it tomorrow... Urquhart House, aye. Ta. Bye love."

When Ian returned, Jock was talking to Stuart, without much luck. The old man looked at Stuart in despair as his head swayed and eyes struggled to focus.

"Yer no gonnae be sick are ye son?"

"No," Stuart managed, "I'm okay. Just can't drink like I used to."

"Christ son, I just kept gettin' better at it!" Jock said, and drained his glass.

"Hello Ian, what do ye make of the lovebirds here eh?" Jock

winked and nodded towards Euan and Sharon. She had him cornered against the window now, and he was squirming, but trying to remain polite as she held his arm with one hand while draining a glass of white wine with the other.

Emily left for the bar. The long suffering sister knew only too well that Sharon had to be kept oiled.

Ian laughed, "Well, he's a free agent, after all. I doubt he was expecting to pull quite so quickly mind you!"

Jock laughed and said, "Ian, it was different in my day I tell ye. There was none o' this." He gestured towards Sharon. "Courtship was a long game. A dance. Ye had tae work at it. Nowadays ye just jump intae bed wi' a lassie. Back then, there was a bit more grace aboot people."

Ian nodded, "Aye, I think you're right. I blame the TV. And all this celebrity culture. All these clueless idiots parading around half-naked. News reports about pop-stars I've never heard of, who can't sing, and their latest public break-up. It's not good for kids to see that shite. Instant fame. The pursuit of wealth. Consumption, that's all we're brought up for. It's all so fucking wrong."

"Aye, we see that rubbish at the home. I sit there on a Saturday night, in the lounge, wi' my pals, and we just laugh at how daft folk have become. This country used tae be the greatest in the world. We invented stuff. We wrote books that folk still read tae this day. We were great. Geniuses. Now we're just the same as everywhere else. We exist only tae buy stuff. Capitalism's ruined this world, and this country. Things have tae change Ian, ye know that?" He held Ian's gaze, looking deep into his eyes.

Ian nodded, as sincerely as he could manage, "I do Jock, I do. If it was up to me, we'd wipe out all that crap. Footballers would get paid a normal wage. Bankers would only get fucking bonuses if they managed to make money. Actually, fuck that, they wouldn't get fucking bonuses at all. They already get paid more than everybody else anyway. And to hell with 'scaring away the talent' if that's what they call it. If they're that talented, let them fuck off and wreck another country. The nurses would get the bonuses. And the teachers. The people that actually make a difference to folks' lives. The compassionate people. The carers. Not the fucking salesmen and the marketers and the bankers. I still think we are great Jock, I've got faith in this country..." He put on his best pub-singer voice, "and we can still rise now and be that nation again!"

Someone in the crowd joined in, "that stood against him!"

"Against who!" a crowd at the bar shouted.

"Proud Edward's army," half the pub had joined in, much to the delight of the tourists, "and sent him homewards, tae think again!"

A cheer went up.

"Good lad!" laughed Jock.

Someone was patting Ian on the shoulder when his phone beeped. He checked the screen. Shona had texted him the number for Urquhart House.

"Good man," the stranger said. "Voting 'yes' next week then I take it?"

"Abso-fucking-lutely!" said Ian and shook his hand.

Euan reached for his pint, and Sharon grabbed his hand. "I like you Euan." She smiled, making her eyes as big as possible.

Oh Jesus, thought Euan. This wasn't right. He was still married. Sort of. She was nice enough, Sharon. Certainly had curves in all the right places. Oh shit. Should he? Vicki had left the house. She'd left him. She was at Dick's. Fucking Dick. The drink wasn't helping. Or was it? He looked outside and saw one of Bubbles' crew approach the pub. Wasn't that the one Stuart had been talking to in Deacon Brodie's? They'd already been told they weren't getting in. Why was he back? He sensed trouble.

"Come on baldy, get your coat, you've pulled!" Sharon

tugged at Euan's arm.

"I'm not falling for that one again!" he said, standing and knocking the table, spilling drinks everywhere.

"Fucksake Euan!" Ian cried. Wiping beer off his jeans.

"He's learning," said Jock.

Euan side-stepped past Sharon and said, "Look Sharon, you're lovely, you really are. But I need to, erm, it's just... I'm drunk, you're drunk, we're all drunk..." he waved his hand around in a circle. "And I need the toilet, excuse me."

He staggered off through the crowd and Sharon watched him go. With a sigh, she drained another wine and once again aimed her sights on Stuart.

"Fuck off ya Polish bastard!" Bubbles' mate was arguing with the bouncer again. "Fuckin' come here and take oor fuckin' jobs."

The bouncer was holding him back at arm's length. "Look, walk away, or I'll phone the police. Go!"

Jock had got out of his chair and headed for the door, leaning on his stick. Ian stood, "Jock, where are you going?"

"Tae help a fellow man," he replied.

Ian stood and grabbed Jock by the arm. "Don't be daft, the bouncer will deal with it!"

A gasp went up and someone shouted, "Oh god he's got a knife!"

Ian let go of Jock and stepped to the side to get a better view out of the window.

He saw Bubbles' mate swing his blade at the bouncer. It was a short combat knife, but the bouncer managed to avoid it and grabbed his arm. He had one hand on his shoulder now, trying to keep him back, and the other holding the knife arm.

A circle of tourists stood on the pavement watching, slack-jawed. Some of the men were making moves to step forward but were being held back by their partners.

A well placed kick, square in the bollocks and the bouncer

collapsed to the ground. The crowds of tourists, still milling around didn't know what to do. They stood, appalled at what was happening in the middle of this beautiful street, in this beautiful city. How could this horror be unfolding in front of them? They'd been watching fire-eaters on unicycles ten minutes ago, and now this! The young guy spat, dancing like a boxer, and screamed, "Fucking wanker, fucking Polish wanker!" and drew his knife arm back. In an instant, he moved to stab the bouncer as he lay on the ground.

He didn't get a chance, as Jock's walking stick cracked the side of his head and sent him sprawling to the pavement.

Ian looked to the side. The old bugger had sneaked off while he was watching the action.

Jock kicked the knife away and asked the bouncer, who was kneeling now, holding his aching balls, "Are you okay son?"

"Yes, thank you," he said, looking at the old man with utter gratitude. "How old are you?"

"Ninety-five son, but eighteen on the inside."

A policeman hurried through the crowd and handcuffed the attacker. His colleague quickly asked some tourists what had happened. "Did you hit him sir?" she asked Jock.

"I did aye," said Jock proudly.

"Well I'll need your name and address. We'll need to take a statement at the station if you don't mind."

"Nae bother dear, John Smith. Urquhart House care home. I'll pop in tomorrow if that's okay?"

She jotted down the details and handed Jock a slip of paper, "Yes that's fine. He's still alive, you're in luck. Here's an incident number. If you could hand that in when you arrive, that'd be great. Just go to your nearest police station in the morning."

"I will do dear," Jock said, then turned and walked back into the pub as the crackle of the police walkie talkie announced that a car was on its way.

"That stick of yours is pretty handy," laughed Ian, meeting

Jock at the door.

"I cannae abide that shite son. Racial intolerance has nae place in this country. We fought beside the Polish in the war and I wouldnae have cared if that bouncer had been a German, I'd still have helped him."

"Sit yourself down Jock, I think we're moving on anyway. One for the road, then we'll get you home okay?"

"One more aye, or maybe two?" said Jock as he sat back down to a hero's welcome from Sharon, Emily and Stuart.

Euan stared at his reflection in the large gilt-edged toilet mirror. That was a close one, he thought. He didn't need another alcoholic nutter like Sharon in his life. He splashed some water on his face and over his head. Pretty steaming now, Euan old boy. Keep it together. And mustn't let Ian get back onto politics, it was getting exhausting. He thought of his flat. It'd be empty. She'd be gone; her stuff would still be there, but this was the beginning of the end. The proper end. It'd been ending for years, their marriage, but once she'd moved out he could start afresh. He'd paint the walls white. Chuck out all the crap he didn't need. Get back to basics. What about work though? She'd still be there. Crap. A new job. That's what he needed. Take redundancy and get the fuck out of there. He'd plenty money in the bank, he could afford to take a few months off. Maybe travel, or start a hobby. Fishing, or golf, or hill-walking. Something that got him out of that fucking house and into the fresh air. The years ahead were suddenly filled with promise, excitement, potential. He could be anything he wanted to be! Christ, this was making him dizzy. He looked at the skinny, bald man staring back at him in the mirror. That was the man he'd become, that other man. The man he'd seen in the mirror all these years, not the one inside his fucking head, with the doubts, the guilt, and the misery. It was time for a change. A new beginning!

He bumped his way happily through the crowd to his friends,

just as a suited youth was being bundled into the back of a police car outside, its lights filling the pub with a flickering blue glow.

"Have I missed something?"

Ian filled Euan in on Jock's heroics while Sharon did her best to persuade Stuart to go home with her.

"Oh come on you gorgeous devil. I'll be gone on Monday. It's not like we'll see each other again. Just a bit of fun. Come on...." She leaned in for a kiss. Stuart winced and wrenched his head away.

God, please leave me alone, Stuart thought. She wasn't his type. In the broadest sense possible. Christ he was drunk now. Really losing it. He was used to a few drinks at night. Not a session like this. He felt sick. Sweaty. She was still grabbing at him. She had her hand on his trousers now. She was bloody insistent, he'd give her that much. But that was all he would give her.

"Look, Sharon," he shoved her away, "you're wasting your time."

"Oh I can be very persuasive," she said, in a voice that she thought sounded like Marilyn Monroe but came across more like Dot Cotton.

"No, believe me, you can't," said Stuart, edging away.

"Stuart, look at me, I like you!" she said, trying the same wide-eyed tactic that had failed so dramatically on Euan, who, along with Ian was watching the action unfold now. They could barely contain their enjoyment at Stuart's predicament.

"Well, I've got news for you. I don't like you."

"You'll grow to like me," she said, as seductively as she could manage - pressing her hand against his crotch.

"Oh I won't, believe me." Stuart attempted to wriggle out of her grasp.

"You will Stuart, everyone likes me eventually." Then, in a baby voice, with a sad lip and hang-dog expression, "How can you not like me Stuart?"

"Because... because I like men!" Stuart shouted.

Ian sprayed beer all over the table. Euan's pint fell from his hand and smashed on the floor.

Sharon stepped back, stared at him for a moment, then said, "Oh, I get it. God that is such a desperate excuse." She pushed him back. "That's pathetic, really. Well you know what, you can just fuck off! And your little bald friend." She scowled at Euan, turned and stomped back to her sister, who didn't look entirely delighted to see her return.

There was a moment's silence while Euan looked at Ian, who looked at Jock, who appeared to be nodding off again.

"Right, erm, I think we're done here," said Ian. "Where's next?"

Outside, they stood for a moment. The police car was still there. The driver was speaking on his radio. Jock was still in the pub, leaning on his stick and chatting to a tourist who'd asked him about his heroics earlier.

Euan said, "Umm, World's End?"

"Very appropriate," said Stuart, his voice slurred and distant.

"Come on mate, a coke will do you good."

Stuart laughed, "Oh yes it would."

"Listen Stuart, that thing you said in there, you meant it aye?"

"Yes Ian. I meant it. I'm gay. I'm fucking gay! I'm a big gay homosexual. What do you think of that?"

"Brilliant. We've been thinking it for years. Or at least I have. Euan wasn't convinced though. Anyway, glad to hear it from the big gay horse's mouth, so to speak!"

Stuart staggered back, "Eh? You've known? Since when?"

Ian stroked his beard and said, "Well, since about three weeks into university, if I'm honest. Come on man, you had every girl in the union after you. We were in awe. And fucking livid at the same time, 'cos you'd always fuck off home alone. As would we, but we had no fucking choice in the matter."

Euan offered, "If it's any consolation, I didn't think you were. Not that that'll be a consolation, but you know what I mean." He kept digging, "I mean I'm happy that you are. No, I'm not happy, I just couldn't give a shit. Not like that, like, I give a shit. I'm happy for you. I just thought you were a fussy bastard that's all. But aye, now that you've said it. Aye, that explains a few things." He laughed and grabbed Stuart's arse. "Come on big boy, let's get you sobered up."

Stuart looked at his friends and thought, shit - all these years of secrecy. Years of locking it away. Hiding in France, is that what he was doing? Was it all a great big fucking cover up? Not any more. Holy shit. What a release. And they didn't seem bothered. Did he think they would be bothered? He wasn't sure. He was so fucking pished right now. He loved these guys. Not in that way. Big manky-bearded Ian and wee bald runty Euan. Not his types. No, no way. Fuck, this was a new beginning for him. Out. Well, he was already out in France. And his Mum knew. And it would appear Ian had known too. What a weight off. He'd been struggling with it. He was planning on telling them on this trip. But not like that. He'd pictured a more sober annunciation, not blurting it out in a packed pub with a drunken woman rubbing his fucking crotch.

Ian watched Jock smile and shake hands with the tourists in the pub as he tried to leave, then took his phone out. He dialled the number for Urquhart House.

As it rang, he saw a girl in a yellow jacket climb into a cab opposite. Hadn't he seen her somewhere before?

The police car drove off down the High Street just as Jock emerged from the pub.

"Hello..." Ian turned away from Jock, "Yes, I'm just calling about one of your residents... Jock, don't know his second name... Ninety-five... red tartan trousers... no, he's fine, he's having a drink with us... he hasn't mentioned any medication no... we don't know him, well we didn't before today... look he's just after a bit of a break as far as I can tell... had some business at the castle... honestly, he's okay... well we're going to have one more drink then I'll get him in a cab... Marchmont, yes I know... okay, will do. Bye."

Ian selected Shona's text and quickly replied, 'Thx. Luv U. Ixxx'. He stuck his phone back in the breast pocket of his jacket and turned back to his friends.

Jock was rubbing his hands together. "Right, I think I need a drink after all that!"

CHAPTER TEN

Rosie

Rosie reached the High Street again and looked over to Cockburn Street. There was a pub near the top, seemed like Jock's type of place. She crossed and opened the door of The Scotsman's Lounge.

The place was fairly quiet. With no sign of Jock. The barman handed some change to a customer and nodded towards her, "Yes?" he smiled.

Rosie was running out of energy now. That call had really taken it out of her. "Oh, I'm looking for a man," she said, with an air of dejection. The barman laughed and said, "Look no further!" he opened his arms towards her.

Rosie laughed and said, "A bit older than you I'm afraid. Ninety-five. Red tartan trousers."

"You've got very specific tastes," he joked.

"Oh god I'm knackered. Can I have a gin and tonic please?" She sat at a bar-stool.

"Sure," he said, grabbing a glass.

Rosie was in two minds now. She wanted to find Jock, to get his medication to him, but part of her now wanted to stick it to

Fraser as much as possible. And a missing person report would certainly help. Okay, it wasn't exactly the home's fault. The guests were free to come and go, but procedures had been missed. Jock had absconded without the necessary paperwork, or a chaperone, and a little thing like that could do a lot of damage to a place's reputation. She was sure Jock was fine. He'd probably roll up to the home in a cab later on. He'd just wanted to visit the museum, and had met a friend for a pint, then latched onto these younger guys. He was like that, Jock. Loved to talk. She laughed at the thought of his speech on The Mercat Cross. He'd be okay. It was Fraser that was at the forefront of her mind now, that smug, arrogant, arsehole. Bought the home with the massive inheritance he'd received from his wealthy parents, who were very much part of the Edinburgh establishment apparently. And what had Fraser done to deserve this? Nothing but be fortunate enough to be born into it.

The barman presented her with a gin and tonic, complete with umbrella and a fresh slice of lemon.

"Oh thanks," said Rosie, smiling, "that's lovely."

"You look like you need cheering up," said the barman.

Rosie explained Jock's disappearance. "I've been hunting high and low for him, just about ready to give up though."

"Well one thing my old mum always told me is that quitters never win," said the barman, pulling a pint for another customer. "Which is why I'm still working in a bar, obviously."

"Because you want to be the world's best barman?" joked Rosie.

"Exactly," he laughed.

Rosie grabbed a newspaper and sat scanning through the small ads at the back. The vacancies section was tiny. There were plenty ads for Staffordshire Bull Terriers, but none for bloody jobs. This was useless. She read the main articles. They were all about the referendum next week. Did she think they'd get it? Independence? It was hard to tell, and she wasn't sure what her views were. Part of her thought it'd be nice for Scotland to be independent. And it wouldn't really affect her anyway. In fact, she thought even more of her friends would probably make the trek north. Things were pretty bleak down there. A fresh start would be good for a country. Exciting. She was sure Scotland could survive on tourism alone. With the scenery, the lochs, the mountains, the rivers, the myths and this amazing capital city, how could they fail? Midges, that's how, she thought, and laughed to herself. Yes, they'd need to sort the midges out first.

She sipped on her gin and looked at the barman. He was nice, maybe he'd ask her for her number. Isn't that how it worked? She asked for another gin and tonic.

"You're thirsty," he said, grabbing a fresh glass.

"It's hard work, geriatric hunting," she said.

He laughed again. This was going well, she thought. He thinks I'm funny. She realised she was slouching and straightened up on her stool, flicking her hair back - one strand had got stuck on her cheek. She caught her reflection in a mirror behind the bar. Not too bad, Rosie, she thought. She licked her lips and glanced again at the barman. He was about thirty, same as her. Nice figure, although she didn't always go for the muscly types. No beer-gut; that was a bonus. Was he the outdoor type? She stood up on the stool's foot rest and stretched over for a look at his shoes. She couldn't quite see them, if she just leaned a little bit further...

With a clatter, the stool shot backwards and she fell forward onto the bar, knocking her remaining gin over. The stool rolled slowly on its side into the middle of the floor.

"Oops," she said, trying for brevity.

"Erm, they can be a bit tricky, those stools," said the barman, bringing her a fresh drink.

Rosie picked up the stool and set it back at the bar. The small crowd were watching her every move, trying not to laugh. She was conscious now of her every move.

She sat back down and took the gin. Her face was burning. The blood rushing to her cheeks. God Rosie you are such a bloody idiot! She buried her face in the newspaper. Half past nine now. Thirty minutes until she phoned the police. She thought about what she'd say to them, anything to take her mind off the crushing embarrassment she was feeling. She heard the door open behind her, and the rumble of a taxi's engine as it drove off down Cockburn Street.

"Hi honey!"

"Hiya love!" the barman said to the tall brunette who had just walked in. He leaned over the bar and kissed her on the lips.

She sat beside Rosie, "What a day. I need a drink. Chardonnay please lover, the bigger the better."

Rosie sighed and drained her glass.

She stood on the pavement, looking down Cockburn Street. Waverley Station was just beyond. What if Jock had got on a train? It didn't bear thinking about. But the police would issue a missing person bulletin. He'd be spotted, either by a conductor, or at a station somewhere.

There was another pub at the bottom of Cockburn Street that was worth a try, the Malt Shovel. Also several beyond that, on Market Street, that he'd be likely to head for, but she knew the chances were slim. Twenty minutes now until she called the police. She tried the Malt Shovel with no luck. This was pointless. She was knackered, and miserable. She'd failed.

She headed back up Cockburn Street. There was a taxi rank on the next stretch of the High Street, outside that big hotel that she could never remember the name of. She'd wander up and get a cab back to the home. Fraser would probably still be there - he'd be waiting to see what her next move was. She wanted to see his face as she called the police and told him she was leaving.

At the top of Cockburn Street she stood for a moment and

scanned the crowds again one last time. They were thinning out now. The holidaying families of the afternoon were being replaced by the evening crowds, heading en masse to the bars and cafes and restaurants. There was no sign of a ninety-five year old man in red tartan trousers. She heard a police siren, a patrol car speeding down South Bridge and onto the High Street. Here we go, she thought. The idiots who can't have a drink without taking a swing at someone. She crossed over and took her place in the taxi rank where a cab arrived almost immediately. The group in front of her climbed aboard. She moved to the head of the rank to wait for the next cab.

The police car had stopped outside a pub opposite, The Mitre. She watched as a policewoman bundled a young lad in a suit into the back of the car. Probably just battered some poor tourist unconscious. She was angry now. What bloody purpose did these young idiots serve? Just a burden on a decent society, she thought. Jock had fought in wars for the freedom of people he'd never met. And had been awarded two bloody great medals for bravery in the process. What would this young idiot ever contribute to society other than anger and misery and heartache for his victims?

A cab pulled up to the head of the rank and with one last and fruitless look up and down the High Street for an old man in red tartan trousers she opened the cab's rear door and climbed in.

"Urquhart House in Marchmont please," she sighed as she flopped into the seat. The cab driver pushed the button on the meter.

"Looks like trouble there eh?" he said, inclining his head towards The Mitre.

"Yeah," said Rosie as the police car pulled away in the opposite direction.

CHAPTER ELEVEN

The World's End

They staggered on, Stuart helped along by Euan, and Jock hanging onto Ian, as they continued down the Royal Mile, past more cashmere shops.

"Do you know anybody that wears cashmere?" asked Euan.

"Can't say I do," said Ian. "And I'm not that keen on shortbread either."

"Do you have a claymore above your mantelpiece?"

"Nope, neither do I have a tartan knee blanket."

"Have you ever drunk whisky from a quaich?"

"No, I use a Tesco tumbler."

"It's good all this shit though isn't it?"

"It appears to be popular, there's a fucking mile of it."

As the pavement narrowed, Jock let go of Ian's arm and climbed some steps at the side of a building.

"Where are you going Jock? That's John Knox's house. The pub's down here," said Euan, pointing down the road towards the World's End.

Jock slowly climbed three steps, then turned. "I just want tae say thank you," he said, leaning on his stick. "I came oot here today tae take care o' a couple o' things. I didnae bank on bumping intae you three. But I'm glad I did." He was drunk now, Ian could see it. He was struggling to keep it together.

He continued, "Stuart, you're a good laddie and I'm glad ye've sorted out whatever it was ye needed tae sort out. Happiness is the one thing in life that cannae be bought or sold, so those buggers cannae control it." He pointed skywards. "If ye can find true happiness in yer life, ye'll be wealthier than the richest banker on Earth and I think you're well on yer way. And feel free tae thank me, 'cos that ruined house ye bought was probably a result o' one of my misplaced shells in 1944."

"Merci beaucoup Jock!" Stuart said.

Jock turned to Euan, "And you son, ye've no' had it easy, but it sounds tae me like ye've turned a corner. Dinnae live yer life lying tae yersel'. Listen tae this..." he patted his heart. "It speaks tae ye in a language that only you can understand. Pay attention tae it, and ye'll live a long and happy life. If ye ignore what it's trying tae tell ye though, ye'll be damned miserable. It sounds like ye've got rid of one problem in yer life, so have a wee think." He pointed at him. "Maybe it's time tae ditch another marriage that ye seem so keen on? What dae ye think?"

Euan shrugged. "Maybe Jock, maybe." Christ, here we go again, he thought. Still, the new Euan, you never know. Was his heart fluttering a bit? Was there a new passion there? He wasn't sure. Could've been the chips from earlier.

Jock continued, "And Ian, despite lookin' like a Russian peasant, you seem tae have yersel' sorted oot. Ye've fathered children, and that's the greatest gift a man can get, but also the greatest burden. Yer children are the future o' this country, and whatever happens next week, make sure ye encourage them tae have the same belief and passion ye carry yersel'. If it doesnae happen this time. It'll happen the next. Make them proud o' their country. Teach them about their history. There's far too many folk out there that have lost track of what it means tae be

Scottish. They just want tae be the same as everybody else, and everywhere else. Well this country isnae the same. It never has been. And it shouldnae be. Can ye promise me that?"

"Of course Jock," said Ian, "I wouldn't have it any other way."

"Good, right. Let's get a drink. World's End ye say? That sounds like a cheery wee place."

They took a corner table in the World's End, named after the narrow close alongside. Back when the population of Edinburgh was huddled together on this long high ridge, there really was nothing beyond the old city walls that concerned them, hence the name.

They were removing their jackets when Jock announced, "I'll get this one, what are ye all having?"

Ian and Euan shared a smile, about time too you tight old git!

"A pint of 80' please Jock," said Ian.

"I'll go back on the Guinness I think," said Euan.

"Stuart will have a coke, I think, Stuart?" Ian looked at his pal. He just grinned dopily back and nodded. "I'll give you a hand."

While Jock and Ian were at the bar, Euan put his hand on Stuart's shoulder and said, "Look Stuart, I'm pleased for you. I mean, it's a bit weird like, especially as we've known you all these years. You should have told us earlier. I couldn't care less if you're gay, straight or a fucking elephant."

"And what would that have achieved?" asked Stuart.

"Well, we might not have let you walk behind us so much!" Euan ducked backwards as Stuart took a jokey swing at him.

"You know Euan, it's been fucking impossible coming back here and living this lie. I go out in France, meet blokes, it's fine. Nobody knows me. Then I come back here and it's all fucking football and tits."

"We haven't mentioned football all night. Or tits."

"Oh come on, that's only cos we've bumped into Jock. The football talk would have started by the second boozer otherwise."

Ian and Jock returned with the drinks.

Euan sat back, and said, "So, Ian, what about The Old Firm meltdown? That's a laugh eh? Fucking tits!"

Stuart shook his head and smiled.

"Peculiar choice of phrase Euan, but aye. Entertaining for the rest of us I suppose. Fucking Glasgow. Does my head in. If they'd stop fighting other people's battles we might have more of a chance of a 'yes' vote next week. You've got one half of the city wrapped in the butcher's apron, banging on about "never ever ever being slaves" while happily being slaves to the fucking monarchy. And the other half are more interested in freedom for Ireland, Palestine, and Catalonia. Couldn't care less about the fucking country they live in."

Jock piped up, "It's their roots son. It's here," he patted his heart, "for both sides. And they're as big a part of Scotland as the rest o' us. I should know, I grew up there. If we dinnae get the vote next week, well, maybe it just wasn't to be. I hope the rest o' us stand up though. We've battled for the right to vote, and there's nothing worse than folk that dinnae use it."

"Hear hear," said Euan. "I've never missed an election, or a local election, or a council vote in my life."

"Aye well the way you're voting you might be better staying in the hoose." Jock said with a chuckle.

"You're from Glasgow?" Ian asked.

"Aye, born 31st January 1919. Black Friday. Glasgow Royal Infirmary. My mother's waters broke and she walked to the hospital through all the chaos that was going on around her."

"Black Friday?" asked Euan. "Was that the stock market collapse?"

"No, Black Friday was a riot son."

"I've heard about it Jock," Ian said. His History degree wasn't completely wasted. "Two years after the Russian revolution.

They were shitting themselves that there was going to be a Bolshevist uprising in Glasgow. There was a day of strike action, 60,000 workers, and it ended in a running battle between police and the marchers in George Square. They shipped in a load of soldiers and tanks to line the streets for weeks afterwards."

"That's right, and do ye ken how the riot started?"

"Didn't the police charge the marchers with batons?"

Jock said, "Well, that's the official story aye, but according to my father, it was only after he chucked a bottle at them."

"That wouldn't surprise me one bit," laughed Ian. "So, your mother walked through a riot to get to the hospital, then what?"

"She walked home again to get my father's tea on. I got to stay in the hospital for a bit, as far as I know."

Ian shook his head, laughing, "I can believe that. And did she get his tea on the table?"

"She did, but she needn't have bothered. He didnae get oot the jail for a month."

They all laughed, joined by some drinkers at the next table who'd been listening in to Jock's story.

"So when did you move through here?" asked Ian.

"Och we lived all over the place after that son. My father took us anywhere there was work. And there wisnae a lot of that going around back then. We were between the wars. The recession was on, and that was a proper recession. No this rubbish they're calling a recession these days." He waved dismissively. "We had cardboard boxes for shoes. We never went back to Glasgow though."

He coughed and gripped the table.

"You okay Jock?" Ian asked, placing his hand on his shoulder.

"Aye, just that whisky. Must have gone doon the wrong way. I'm fine."

"There's still kids wearing cardboard for shoes these days Jock." Ian said, "It's hard to believe. Folk are relying on fucking handouts from foodbanks. Fourth most unequal country in the world we're in now. And a lot of it's evident in your home city. Yet some of the fucking idiots will still vote no next week. If they vote at all."

Euan's phone chirped. He took a drink of his pint as he checked the screen. He paused with the glass at his lips. It was another text message from Vicki: 'Euan, I'm so sorry. We can work it out. Call me. V.'

Oh for fuck's sake.

Euan stood to leave, "I need to make a call."

Jock said, "And I need a pish, you two behave yerselves now." He winked at Stuart.

"He's safe Jock, don't worry," said Stuart.

Euan stepped outside. It was relatively quiet down at this end of the High Street. There was a burst of laughter from the pub opposite. A taxi sped past hurrying through the traffic lights before they changed. He was alone as he breathed deeply and stared down Canongate. The last stretch of The Royal Mile. This was his route home. Down that narrow, dark canyon of a road.

This was the edge of the city in times gone by. The old Flodden Wall was long gone, but down that road had always lain danger, and the unknown.

He thumbed through his phone's 'favourite numbers'.

There it was: 'Vicki'. He pressed her name on the screen.

"Hello... Uhuh... Where?... Well if you're at Dick's why don't you stay there?... No... No Vicki... Look... Calm down... There's no point that's why... Because, as you said yourself, it's over... it is... it is... no it is... we both know it... You can't mess me around like this... I know, but that was your decision too you know... don't try and blame me for everything... listen, I couldn't care less... I'll re-mortgage and give you half... seriously... look, Dick's giving you what you want, you'll be a mum... well she'll grow to like you... she will... give it time... she will... you'll be a family... we could never be a family... I don't want to, you know that...

Vicki, we're finished, we can either make it messy, or make it easy... I know... well it's not fucking easy for me either you know, you're the one that's been fucking around... I'm okay... I really am okay... no of course I'm not fucking happy, I'm just okay. What do you want me to say? Beg you to come back to me?... no... phone me tomorrow, we'll sort it out... I'll start packing your stuff... Work?... I'll start looking for another job... yes... I feel like a change anyway... look, I'm going back into the pub now... no... definitely not... I'm sorry... Hello?"

There was a click, then silence.

The sound of laughter was still coming from the pub across the road. A car stopped at the lights in front of him, its passenger glancing his way. He could hear the buzz of the city all around him and the beating of his heart in his chest.

"Well done son," he jumped at the sound of Jock's voice.

"Jeeso Jock, I nearly shat myself there. What are you doing out here?"

"Just came oot for some air. Listen, I heard yer conversation there. Ye're doing the right thing. Listening to this," he placed his hand on his heart. "And better still, ye've learnt from your mistakes." He grabbed Euan's shoulder. "You just need to sort your politics oot now."

Euan looked skywards, "Aye Jock, come on. Let's get the round in."

"Pint of Guinness, pint of 80', a coke and whatever your malt of the month is please," Euan asked the barman.

"Guinness is off, sorry. The pressure's gone. We've got bottles."

"Aye that's fine," said Euan, turning to watch Jock hobble back to the table. He had really warmed to this old man today, and they'd only been out for, what, he checked his watch - the red LED read 22:45 - just under six hours. What a difference a few hours can make. He was now single; he was facing an unknown future; one of his best mates was gay; and they'd met a war hero. This was a pub crawl to be remembered.

Stuart passed, on his way to the toilet.

"Another coke okay Stuart?"

"Aye, cheers," then, "fuck it, no, stick a vodka in it too."

"Good man," said Euan and asked the barman, "Did you get that?"

"Yeah," the barman said, then, "sorry. 80's off too. All the draught stuff's gone." He started dropping plastic tumblers over the top of the pump handles.

Euan sighed, "okay, just a bottle of something. Whatever your most rancid real ale is, that'll do. The chewier the better."

The barman laughed and looked in the fridge, pulling out a black bottle with a thistle on the label. A craft beer from one of the many micro-breweries that were popping up all over Scotland. "This stuff's an acquired taste." He read the label, "Coconut, toffee, woodsmoke, berries and spices combine... blah blah blah, this do?"

"Has it got penicillin and mouthwash in it too? Aye that's fine."

"Here we go, draught's all off so I got you this." He presented Ian with the craft beer.

Ian perused the label, "Sounds nice. Ta. See, another growth industry in Scotland. We're already world leaders of the whisky world, no reason we can't wipe the floor with the beer market too."

"It's no oil though is it?" argued Euan.

"Oil's dying Euan. But long before it runs out, we'll have moved onto renewable energy anyway. If we keep our hands on the oil revenue that's left. And it's a shit-load. We could be at the forefront of that too - you might have noticed it's windy as fuck here. We could be providing a quarter of Europe's wind energy. Gold mine."

Euan took a swig of his bottle. Renewable energy? Maybe

he'd get an electric car. Or a hybrid, yes, that'd be better. New car. New life. New Euan. He pictured himself driving all over Scotland with some new woman at his side. She had a head scarf on, like Grace Kelly. And they were enjoying the outdoors, not stuck in his flat staring at other people's miserable lives on the TV.

He took another drink and said, "Aye okay, but give it a rest Ian, please. I don't have the energy. Mine isn't renewable. It's nearly all spent. But aye, I hear what you're saying. Progress, things change. That's why I don't see the point in breaking up the country. We've got enough to deal with without worrying about the logistics of it all. I mean, what money do we use?"

"It really doesn't matter what the fuck we choose to name our beans Euan." Ian said, "and anyway, we're keeping the pound. It's in everyone's interests."

"And what about all the other changes. The Health Service? Defence? Do we get an army?"

"Of course we will, but we'll get rid of Trident first. And we'd save enough to build 20 fucking schools in the process. And our Health Service has been protected by the Scottish Government, and would continue to be. NHS is fucked in England; the bastards have broken it up for privatisation - passed a vote in the House of Lords, where many of the fuckers stand to make a personal fortune out of it. Do you not think Westminster is a fucking stinking hole of corruption?"

Euan shook his head, "It's just too big a job. Do you know how hard it is for me to make one tiny change to the systems at my work? I need to fill out forms, get them signed, wait for approval, schedule the work, make the change, test the change, then it sits there for fucking ages before it gets applied. Christ, if we get independence, I'll need to change all the 'Country' drop-down menus in our web pages. We'll need to add 'Scotland' to the list. It'd be a nightmare."

"A nightmare? Really?" Ian said, taking a large swig of his

beer and staring at Euan. He shook his head.

Stuart returned from the toilet, shaking his hands dry, "Hand drier's knackered."

Jock drained his whisky and sat quietly, Ian watched him while Stuart and Euan joked about wind-powered cars. Jock was looking knackered now, slouched in his chair. They really needed to get him home.

"Come on lads, drink up. I think we need to get Jock home. Or I can just go up with him, should make it back for last orders," he checked his watch.

Jock straightened up, "No, dinnae be daft. I'm fine. There's another pub down the road I'd like to visit, just a quick one for the road?"

Ian thought for a minute. He'd planned this pub crawl carefully. It was no coincidence they'd end up outside the Scottish Parliament at the foot of The Royal Mile. He'd hoped the route would have helped persuade Euan to change his voting intentions. Set the scene, get him drunk in Edinburgh's most tartan and tourist laden street, niggle away at his doubts, and end with a grandstand finish outside the building where all the decisions could be getting made. Instead of just the little ones they let them play around with.

"One more Jock, seriously. You're looking done in," said Ian.

"I've never felt better," said Jock with a smile.

They drained their drinks and headed for the door, Ian helping Jock out of his seat.

"I'll get ye ootside. It's a long walk, and I need another pish," Jock said.

Ian, Euan and Stuart stood at the crossroads outside the World's End. The streets were dark now, and the Canongate stretched out ahead of them on its long, slow descent to the Parliament and the Palace of Holyrood.

This last stretch of the Royal Mile was quieter than the rest, the cashmere shops slowly losing ground to more cerebral retailers selling antique maps and books. The shops were all closed now, and there were precious few pubs so there was a deserted air about the road ahead.

Jock looked at himself in the toilet mirror and sighed a long, drawn out sigh. He gripped the edge of the sink momentarily then looked up again at his reflection. Who was that wrinkled, stooped figure looking back at him? The cheeks red with burst blood vessels, and the mess of white hair hanging down the sides - every last piece of pigment gone. He remembered the picture of him and Ellie back in his room at Urquhart House. It was taken the year before she died. They'd been standing in Holyrood Park, with the mountainous bulk of Arthur's Seat behind. It was only 16 years ago but felt like a lifetime. His long incarceration at Urquhart House had aged him more than the 54 years they'd been married, that was for sure. He still felt like a young man when that photograph was taken, despite being nearly 80. That was Ellie's doing. She had kept him young. Young at heart anyway. He cried at the memory of the woman he'd loved and whispered her name.

He turned on the tap and washed the tears from his face. Then hit the button on the hand-drier. Nothing. He tutted and shook his hands dry. "Does nothing bloody work anymore?"

He returned to the buzz of the bar. He checked that his three companions were out on the pavement before nodding to the barman, "Four whiskies please, doubles, Highland Park, 18 years."

The barman collected four glasses, "They're coming back in then? I thought you'd left?"

Jock just nodded and handed over the money, a £50 note, "Keep the change son."

He drained the whiskies one after the other and headed outside.

CHAPTER TWELVE

Rosie

Rosie climbed the steps to Urquhart House, she sighed at the sight of the place. Happy memories of Jock battled in her head with the anger she felt towards Fraser. She would have to leave after his threat, wouldn't she? How could she keep working for that bloody arrogant fool?

She checked the staff car park and was pleased to see his Land Rover was gone. At least she wouldn't have to deal with him tonight. But that was so typical of him; buggers off home while one of his residents is still wandering the streets.

Sheila met her at the door, "Good news, I was just about to call you but Maisie had a bit of an accident," she pointed at her backside and held her nose, "Jock's okay!"

"Oh thank God! How do you know?"

"Someone called at about ten, said they were out for a drink with him, and that they'd bring him home soon. Before midnight probably. They were just having another drink."

"That's good, but what about his tablets?"

"They said he was fine, he'd been doing something at the castle, then he'd gone for a drink. They'd met him, and gone on a bit of a pub crawl. Sounded fine. Friendly like. I don't think there's anything to worry about."

"Sheila, you don't know the half of it," she laughed. "Stick the kettle on and I'll fill you in on what our old friend's been up to."

CHAPTER THIRTEEN

The Canongate

Jock came clattering out of the pub, falling over the step. Ian grabbed him, "Whoa Jock, steady there. You okay?"

"I just tripped over the step there," said Jock. "Come on, let's get goin', it's a long way to the next drink."

"What pub did you have in mind?" asked Ian.

"It's right doon at the bottom of the mile," said Jock. "Give me a hand here." He leaned on Ian for support.

"Right, lead on Macduff," he pointed his stick down the Canongate.

"Actually lads, I think I'm going to head home now," said Stuart. "I'm trollied. And all this confessing has taken it out of me. Just need my kip now."

He couldn't be convinced otherwise, so Ian said, "Okay mate, well it's been a blast. Come here." He hugged Stuart who, for the first time, hugged him back, giving him a few hefty slaps on the back.

Jock leaned against the pub wall while Euan shook Stuart's hand and said, "Don't be a stranger, seriously. Don't just disappear to France. Keep in touch eh? You're welcome at my place anytime."

"Thanks Euan, and likewise, come over whenever you like. The wine's cheap, and the weather's great. You're all welcome. You too Jock. I'm sure they'd love your stories down at the Tabac."

Jock nodded and said, "Aye son, but I think my travelling days are over."

Stuart continued, more awkwardly, "And thanks, like, for not freaking out at my revelation. I wasn't really planning it like that. Well, I was hoping the opportunity might have come up. But not like that. Suppose it was a stroke of luck I bumped into mad Sharon on the train eh?"

"Things happen for a reason," Euan said, with an air of the philosopher about him.

"Check out David Hume here," laughed Ian. "So, last piece of business Stuart. Are you voting next week?"

"Of course I am Ian, got the postal ballot in my flat. I'll send it first thing Monday morning."

"And you'll be voting....?" Ian stared at Stuart, eyebrows raised.

"Yes, Ian, I'll be voting, yes." He hailed a passing cab. It stopped alongside, engine rumbling as Stuart opened the door.

"You mean 'yes, I'll be voting' or 'I'll be voting yes?'" Ian asked, as Stuart pulled the door closed.

"Figgate Street please," he said to the driver, then shouted out the window, "Right see you guys again. Great meeting you Jock. Ian, I'll be voting yes."

"Did that have a comma before the 'yes'?" Ian wasn't giving up.

Stuart just laughed as the taxi drove off into the night.

"Heads on sticks Ian," Jock said, pointing upwards.

"Eh? Where?" said Ian.

"Used to be here, the old city gates, the Netherbow Port. See those brass things in the road?"

Ian and Euan looked down. There were numerous brass blocks inlaid into the cobbles.

Jock continued, "That's where the gate was. They'd stick the heads o' criminals up on the battlements. Up there," he pointed upwards again, into the sky. "Heads on sticks."

They headed into the dark Canongate, Jock leaning on Euan now while Ian called home.

"Hi love, it's me... what you up to?... that's the worst film ever... yes I am fairly drunk now... it's been quite a night... well, we've been joined by a war hero, who's also a fairly good politician, a surgeon and an inventor, oh, and not a bad scrapper too... no we weren't fighting, just him... that's the thing, he's ninety-five... I know... did I mention he could drink us under the table?... unreal... god knows, but we've had a skinful... yeah, Urquhart House, thanks for that... that's where he lives... we're having one for the road then I'm taking him up the road in a cab. I'll be home after that okay... how's the munchkins?... awww... right, love ya. I'll see you in a bit... I'll try not to but I might be clumsier than usual... if we had a spare room I could snore the night away in there?... I know... I know... we'll work something out... don't worry about it... right got to go... bye."

Jock had stopped to look at the first pub they were passing, The White Horse. "That's no' right," he said. "The White Horse is further doon, I'm sure."

"We could just have one here?" said Euan. "You'll get home quicker."

"No, let's keep going," Jock said.

"Stuart said you were looking for someone, are they in this pub we're heading to?"

"Did I say that? I think someone's probably more likely tae be lookin' for me. No son, I'm not lookin' for anyone, not any more."

Ian had walked on ahead and paused for a look in a shop

selling old maps. He loved poring over old maps. It was probably why he'd applied for his job at the land registry in the first place. It certainly wasn't for the salary. He thought again about his call to Shona, and her little reminder that they were going to have to move house soon, after the baby was born. He had a year, at most. It looked like they'd need to move out of town to get the extra bedroom and garden they needed. Not the end of the world, he thought, but he loved this city. He loved taking the kids to the castle, or the museum, or the botanics in spring. Their friends were all here, and okay, the majority of his social life these days revolved around dinners at friends' houses, and not nights like this, but he'd miss that. Nobody had the room for a family of five to sleep over, so they'd be relying on taxis out to East Lothian, or wherever they ended up. Would they be any better off, really? They'd be trading so much for that little bit of extra space. He knew Shona felt the same - she was a city girl through-and-through. Give her a decent coffee shop and the company of her friends on a sunny afternoon and she was in heaven.

He looked at the selection of maps propped up on stands in the window. Some showed early outlines of Scotland, sketched by the first cartographers sailing around the coastline. His eyes rested on one from 1708 titled "The Northern Part of Great Britain" - it was a rough, childlike approximation of the nation's shape with unreadable place names in cursive inky scripts. Scotland at the birth of the union, malformed and nameless.

Over the years, the maps began to show more detail. The angles became tighter, the islands more defined, the cuts made by the great rivers of the Forth and the Clyde more accurate, until eventually we'd managed to map our nation with utter precision. He looked at a more recent map, from the 19th Century - it showed the outline of Scotland as we knew it, with forests and hills and the blossoming road and rail network -"A travelling map of Scotland" it was titled.

And the journey's not over yet, he thought.

The only thing that marked this map as an antique, other than the lack of motorways, was that the place names were different. It showed the old county names, like Haddingtonshire and Roxburghshire, the boundaries between them more complex than the simplified council regions of today.

"Come on, Jock's thirsty," said Euan in passing.

"Look at this Euan," Ian said, pointing at the map.

"Uhuh, Scotland, how much is it?"

"I don't want to buy it. Look at the place names."

Euan peered closer for a look, "Aye, the old county names, so?"

"So things can change Euan, it's easy."

"Christ this road goes on for miles," said Euan.

"It goes on for a mile Euan, the clues in the title," said Ian, laughing.

They were passing some gates, flanked by two pointed stone columns when Jock stopped and peered through the ironwork.

"What are you looking for Jock, do you need a pish again?" asked Euan.

"If I could get through these gates I would, aye, and I'd pish all over the place."

"You could just do it here," Ian said. "There's nobody about. No need for your walking stick pish-tube. We'll keep an eye out."

Jock said, "Aye, I will thanks," and unzipped, unleashing a stream of pee through the gates.

"That's for selling us out you fucking rogues," he said as he zipped up.

"Who sold us out?" Euan asked.

"That's where they signed the Treaty of Union son, in 1707. And these gates would have been buckling under the weight of the thousands that were trying to stop them."

"I thought Scotland was happy to join them, we were broke weren't we?"

"Certain individuals might have been, but there was nae public support for it. We were bought and sold, for English gold, as Burns put it. Our trade routes were deliberately crippled. King William was doing his best tae ruin us and force us intae it. He didnae want the French invading England through Scotland. Naebody wanted the union, in Scotland or England. They gathered their armies at the borders - if we hudnae signed it, we'd have been forced intae it under the sword." He shook his head and waved a fist at the gates, "Shower o' bastards!"

"Right, come on Jock. I think they've gone now," Ian said, and took his arm.

"So Jock, you defeated Hitler, then what? Was your money still there when you got back?" Ian asked, as they made their way onwards, down the Canongate.

"Oh aye. Well, my mother and father were at death's door by then, and I wanted them tae see me settle doon. So the first thing I did was marry Ellie. I'd bought them a hoose on the banks of Loch Lomond and we got married in the village church. Ellie's folks were already dead, killed in the Clydebank blitz. So there was just the four o' us there, and an army friend o' mine as a witness."

"What about all your gambling pals, did they not show up?"

"We werenae on speaking terms by then son. Remember I'd bankrupt some o' them," Jock managed a laugh. "One o' them came a cropper near here actually. Got lifted for trying to break in somewhere. Daft bugger. No, I didnae see any o' them when I got back fae the war. Just kept my head doon and started work. I was building a life wi' Ellie, I wanted it tae be on honest foundations."

"So what did you do, for work?"

"Ach, whatever I could. The money lasted for a while, but

there were still mines back then, and factories. I've done it all. Worked doon a mine for 20 years, then got sick of the dark and the cold and the achin' bones so I got a job in one of the new car plants as a machinist. Everybody wanted motors. It was crazy. I stayed there most o' my life. Retired just as Maggie Thatcher was closing them all doon and layin' Scotland to waste."

"Aye I remember it well. My dad got laid off in the 80s. I was ten. We couldn't even afford coffee."

"Well there's worse hardships son," Jock said.

Ian was struck again at how cruel it was that Jock had never managed to have children. He'd devoted his life to Ellie, and by the sounds of it, they'd had a happy life together, but that one thing had eluded them.

"You'd have been a great father Jock," Ian said. "I mean, with your stories, and your sense of right and wrong. It's a real shame you never managed... I'm sorry."

"Och dinnae be sorry son, it's hardly your fault. It just wisnae to be. Ellie and me had a wonderful life together, and we did a lot o' things that we'd never have done if we'd had children. We had holidays," he laughed. "We drove a Hillman Imp right aroond the coast o' Scotland one year."

"Aye well, we could do with a bit of that I suppose," Ian said. "No idea how though, society seems to be set up to make it as hard as possible for people who want to work and have children."

"Aye, financial problems can eat away at a marriage though. Don't let them, do ye hear me? That's the last thing ye should be falling out about."

"We're not falling out over it. We just both know we're struggling that's all."

Jock nodded, then looked upwards, "I stick by this boy's reasoning." He pointed at the side of a building they were passing.

Ian looked up at some gold Latin inscriptions on the wall.

"I am a happy man today, your turn may come tomorrow, so

what's your problem?" Jock exclaimed.

"That's what it says?" Ian asked.

"Aye, roughly. He was worried his fine hoose would get people jealous. It's true though. Ye never know what's around the corner."

"What does that one say?" asked Ian, pointing at another inscription.

"Haud on," said Jock, resting his weight on his stick and peering upwards: "I am old but renew my youth."

He stood for a moment, then looked across the road to the Canongate church, where a man with a dog was heading through the gates.

"I know that man," said Jock. "Hello!"

The man turned to face them, "Fuck sake, I'd know those trousers anywhere. Hello my man. How are you? Did you make it to the castle?"

"Come on lads, meet a friend o' mine," said Jock and hobbled across the road.

Euan stood back, inspecting the stranger. He looked a bit rough, unshaven, dirty hair, and his dog was on a length of rope. There was a bottle of Buckfast sticking out his jacket pocket. Classic jakey, he thought, what are we getting into now?

Ian approached as Jock was saying hello and shaking the man's hand.

"Ian son, this is Alex. A soldier of the Royal Scots Dragoon Guards. Fought in Iraq for a bunch of lying, thieving, crooks and came home tae be chucked on the scrap heap."

Ian and Alex shook hands.

Euan joined and said an awkward "Hello." He almost gagged as he entered the cloud of piss and Buckfast fumes that Alex emanated.

"So, that book you gave me," said Alex, "I met a girl, told me it was worth a lot of money. She wasn't wrong, look," he took out a few crumpled notes. "A hundred quid! Well, there's only fifty left, but no' bad eh? I can't thank you enough my man," he patted Jock on the shoulder.

"Well, I thought it might help ye oot," said Jock, looking downwards.

"It's certainly done that," he said, staggering backwards and patting the Buckfast in his pocket.

"Where did ye sell it?" asked Jock.

"Some place off the Cowgate, don't know the name. Boy in there was chuffed when he saw it like, practically grabbed it out my hands. Offered me sixty quid to start with, but I'm not daft, so I held out for a hundred."

Jock sighed, "You cannae remember the name o' the place?"

"No, I could take you there though. I know the streets. Never forget a doorway."

Jock thought for a moment, "Okay Alex, here's what to do. You wait at Hunter Square tomorrow until one o' these fine lads shows up." He indicated Ian and Euan, who looked at each other in confusion. "And take them tae the bookshop. If they cannae convince the boy to hand it over, you're going to get that book back using yer soldiering skills, you understand?"

"What, batter the guy?"

"Aye son, kick fuck out of him if ye have to, but get that book back. Then ye need tae take it to the regimental museum at the castle. Ask for Major Macpherson, he'll help ye out. Tell him ye want it to go tae auction, have you got that?"

"Aye," said Alex, "Is it worth more than a hundred quid like?"

"I'd expect so son, just make sure ye do this. Promise me."

"Aye, I will," he looked at Ian. "You'll fit in fine with my mates, with that beard. I'll see you tomorrow."

"Erm, aye, okay," said Ian.

"Right, well I'm just away in here for my bed," Alex said, pointing to the churchyard.

"Aye well, they're quiet neighbours, the deceased," Jock said. "Look after yerself son. There's a big grave in there, ye'll recognise the name. Ye might want to raise a glass to the memory of the man that's under it."

"Why's that?" asked Alex.

"He wrote your book," said Jock.

As Alex entered the churchyard he turned and shouted, "Jock, that girl I spoke to, she was looking for you, blonde, good looking. You got a bit on the side?"

Jock shook his head, "No son, just another good Samaritan."

"So who was the girl Jock?" asked Ian.

"It'll be Rosie from the home," Jock said. "She's a good lass. Always lookin' out for me."

"Well you'll see her soon enough, I phoned the home - said we'd get you home after this drink."

"Aye okay son, thanks for doing that. Make sure that boy gets his book back, promise me?"

"Sure Jock, I will, I'll go up tomorrow. So where are we headed?" Ian asked.

"There's an old pub, down at the bottom," Jock replied. "I've no' been there for years, but it's a good wee place for a nightcap. It's been quite a day son, I've had a good time. But it's time to knock it on the head."

"Too true Jock," said Euan. He'd been lost in thought. The crushing reality of his marital situation was beginning to dawn on him. "I think I need my bed fairly soon too."

"Lightweights," said Ian.

Jock started laughing, then stopped immediately. He seized Ian's arm. "Hold me up son, give me a minute."

"Are you sure you're up for this? We can just get a cab back now if you want."

"No, I'm fine. I'm okay," he shook his stick in the direction they were heading. "Onwards."

Ian looked at Jock as they walked. He was more stooped than before, hardly surprising given the amount of whisky he'd consumed but he still walked with some purpose, taking the weight expertly on his stick and keeping the pace. He looked clammy though; beads of sweat were running down his forehead and his thin white hair was sticking to the sides of his head. He had spots of blood on his shirt from his antics in Deacon Brodie's earlier.

Ian thought back over the evening's events. His plans for the night had involved performing a political conversion on Euan, and hopefully swinging Stuart in the right direction. He realised the inappropriateness of that thought and laughed.

"What are you chuckling to yourself about?" asked Euan.

"Nothing, just thinking about Stuart's public outing - I LIKE MEN!"

Euan snorted and laughed heartily, happy to be shaken out of his own thoughts.

Ian looked at his friend as they walked, Jock hobbling along on his arm. Had he done enough to convince him? He'd argued that plenty small countries existed quite happily in Europe, and were in a better financial state than they were. He'd got the stuff about getting rid of Trident in, but had he mentioned a Tory-free future? He'd made his case for taxes not necessarily being a bad thing. He'd reminded him that the economy wasn't wholly reliant on the oil, but what a bonanza we'd have if we got our hands on all the remaining revenue from it. He'd busted the myth that we were being subsidised by Westminster, that it was actually the other way around, hence their desperation to keep the union. He had plenty more ammunition, statistics and figures that proved his arguments held water, but he'd save them for the next pub. Euan liked statistics and figures - the programmer in him needed raw data. He'd tried the emotional argument, now was the time for the nitty-gritty. The head rather than the heart. And where better than the foot of the Royal

Mile, right next to the Scottish Parliament, for his grandstand finish? Euan was on the ropes, he was sure of it. He just needed to finish the job now.

Jock said, "Nearly there, look." He pointed towards the foot of the Royal Mile.

Ian saw that they were passing Queensberry House, now swallowed up by the new Parliament buildings. On the night the resident Duke of Queensberry was up at Moray House putting his signature to the 1707 Treaty of Union, his insane son was roasting a kitchen boy over a spit to have for dinner. "Cannibals," he said, recounting the tale and pointing to the old building, incongruous amongst the modernity of the buildings that surrounded it. "Bloody unionists. They eat children, Euan, you not seeing the light yet?"

Euan shook his head. "No, but you've put me in the mood for a kebab."

They'd reached the sculpted curved walls of the Parliament building, covered with abstract shapes and inset plaques with quotes from Scottish history. You had to hand it to that Spanish architect, this was a building for the future. It had its critics, mainly due to the spiralling costs during its construction, but Ian loved the place. There was nowhere like it on Earth.

Jock slowed down and leant on the wall, catching his breath. He raised a hand to hold Ian's shoulder.

"Look at this," he said, pointing at an inscription on the wall.

Ian read the plaque: "'Work as if you live in the early days of a better nation.' That's good, I like that."

Jock nodded, but said nothing. His lips were pursed together now, and he was breathing deeply through his nose.

"Come on Jock, where's this pub?" Euan asked.

Jock looked up and with a shaky arm, pointed across the road at a whitewashed building. "The White Horse Inn, over there. Help me son."

Ian took his arm again and most of his weight, Jock was leaning heavily against him now.

They took another few steps before Jock stopped again. He was gasping for air.

"Jock, what's the matter?"

Jock struggled for a while to control his breathing, then said, "It's a long journey for an old man."

He stared at Ian. The twinkle in his eyes seemed dulled. His clammy skin seemed greyer than before. The colour was leaving his cheeks. He grabbed Ian's hands and said, "Oh fuck."

"Come on Jock, we'll get you home. Euan, call a taxi, quick!"

Euan pulled out his mobile and stabbed in a taxi number, "Come on.... fucking engaged."

Ian looked around, but there was no sign of a cab. A car crossed the roundabout at the bottom of the Royal Mile, heading towards Abbeyhill, another passed heading into Holyrood Park, but none had the orange roof light they were looking for.

He felt Jock's weight disappear as he collapsed onto the pavement.

"Shit, scrap that Euan. Ambulance! Hurry up!"

"Jock, can you hear me?"

Jocks eyes were staring at some invisible distant point. He was clutching his heart, gasping for air. Ian sat him against the parliament wall and straightened his legs.

"We're getting you an ambulance Jock, okay? You'll be fine. Keep breathing, deep and slow, that's it."

"I'm going son," Jock said, barely audible, "listen to me, this is important." He pulled Ian close.

"There's a box in my room at the home..." he looked at Ian to make sure he'd heard. Ian nodded. "There's two things in there..." he gasped, breathing slowly, trying to keep focused. "Give Rosie... the girl fae the home, Ellie's ring... and there's some paperwork - that's for you, ye'll know what to do with it...

you keep the box... use it to put your new bairn in..."

"Okay," said Ian, his brow furrowed, "but you're going to be fine Jock."

"Ambulance is on its way," Euan said, kneeling alongside. "Come on Jock, I need a pish, we were nearly there too."

Jock managed a smile, "The pub's not there... must have closed... things change eh?..."

Euan smiled, "Yes Jock, after tonight I'm well aware of that. Come on, breathe easy, that's it. Deep breaths."

"Here son, this is for you..." Jock reached into the pocket of his red tartan trousers and pulled out a small bundle of newspaper. He handed it to Euan.

"Thanks, Jock, I don't need anything though. And you're going to be fine. You keep it." He tried to hand it back but Jock waved him away.

They heard an ambulance siren from the other side of the Parliament, speeding through Holyrood Park, filling the air with the sound of hope. Come on, thought Ian, looking to the roundabout at the bottom of the Royal Mile. He saw the blue flicker of flashing lights bounce off the buildings as the ambulance approached.

"It's here, you hold on okay? Look at me Jock..." Ian said.

Jock's head rolled back and hit the wall, he hissed, a terrifying inhuman noise and grabbed Ian again. Saliva bubbled around his lips. "The box... it's locked... the combination is... twenty..." he trailed off, clutching his chest and rolling onto his side. He drew his legs up, like an old leaf curling up at the end of autumn. Oh fuck thought Ian, come on Jock, keep it together.

Jock was whispering something now. Ian had to place his ear against his mouth to hear it against the wail of the siren as it turned the corner. The siren cut out as the driver saw them. All was suddenly quiet as the ambulance skidded to a halt.

"What's that Jock, whose story? What are you saying, it's whose story?"

"His... story... son. I am... his... story..."

Ian grabbed Jock's head, staring into his eyes, but the light had gone out. He seemed to melt into the pavement. He grabbed his hand, cold and clammy.

"Jock?"

A paramedic jumped from the passenger seat.

"Okay guys, step out the way, what's happened?"

Ian and Euan stood. Ian was still holding Jock's hand. He let it go and it fell to the pavement, lifeless.

He stared straight ahead at an inscription on the Parliament's wall. It read, 'Abair ach beagan is abair gu math e - Say but little and say it well.'

"He's history," Ian said.

Passing cars slowed to get a better look. A cab passed, orange "For Hire" light blazing. Every sound seemed amplified, every colour more vivid. They could hear the crackle of the ambulance's radio. The hum of the lights. They smelt the washing powder on the blanket they'd wrapped him in. The blue lights of the ambulance danced off the parliament building and the whitewashed walls of White Horse Close. They were both drunker than they'd been in a long time, but felt like they hadn't touched a drop. The adrenaline seemed to have killed the alcohol in their blood.

They loaded Jock's body into the ambulance. Ian watched the trolley disappear into the fluorescent sanitised interior. Jock was lost under a blanket, barely making an impression on it. He was just flesh and bones now. How could that be? How could that man ever be just flesh and bones? He was alone. He'd arrived alone, and he'd left the world alone. Should he go with him? What purpose would that serve? He's dead. Nothing he could do now would help Jock. He was just a body now. Flesh and bones waiting to be processed through the system. His death registered, his funeral organised. In an instant, he'd gone

Craig Smith

from a thinking, breathing, living thing that could change someone's life, to nothing.

But what a trail he'd blazed in the years of his life, and what a way to spend your last day. Ian felt suddenly guilty. Jock should have been with his family, but he had none. He should have been at the home, with his friends, but he'd chosen to leave. Did he know this was coming? He'd gifted his medals to the castle, given away an antique book and now he wanted Ian to sort out his remaining effects at the home. He'd planned this, Ian thought. The daft old bugger had planned all this.

The paramedic jumped from the back of the ambulance and said, "Can you hit the lights Mark?" The driver flicked a switch, leaving them in the orange glow of the streetlights.

"Are you related to him?" she asked.

"No," said Ian, voice cracking, "we just met him today. He's got no relatives as far as I know. He's a resident of a care home, Urquhart House, in Marchmont."

"Well someone will need to deal with the paperwork I'm afraid. He'll be taken to the city morgue; you'll be able to collect his body there."

"We'll sort it out," said Ian.

The ambulance drove off up the Canongate, leaving the two friends alone at the foot of the Royal Mile. They stood, not knowing what to say.

The roundabout here offered four routes: back up the Royal Mile to the castle, where they'd met just over six hours ago; straight ahead to the gated royal splendour of Holyrood Palace; right to the doors of the Parliament and the rugged peak and jagged edges of Arthur's Seat and Salisbury Crags - Scotland in miniature; and left to Abbeyhill, and eventually the comfort of their homes, where Ian would kiss his children goodnight and climb into bed beside Shona, careful not to wake them in their box-like flat. He thought of the box Jock mentioned, what had he meant by that? 'Put your new bairn in it'? Must be a big box.

And Euan? He would be heading back to an empty flat, poor old Euan, the unluckiest man in Scotland. Or was he? Ian was happy for him. As happy as he could be given the circumstances.

He looked at his friend, pale and thin, his eyes wet with tears. "Fucking hell eh?"

Euan just shook his head. He was still holding the small bundle of newspaper Jock had given him. He unwrapped it carefully, a glimpse of crimson ribbon then a heavy brass cross visible in the folds of the old newspaper.

"Fucking hell, it's his Victoria Cross!" Euan said. Jaw hanging open, he held it up and turned it around, reading the inscription on the back as it swung in his hand: 'FOR VALOUR'.

"He must've liked you after all," said Ian, patting Euan on the back.

Euan smiled, and cradled the medal in his hand. He stared at it, wide-eyed. Jock had single-handedly destroyed a German unit for this. All he'd done was refuse to take his alcoholic wife back. "We'll better get to the home. Tell them the news."

CHAPTER FOURTEEN

Urquhart House

Rosie jumped out of her chair as she heard a taxi stop at the gates, her detective book falling onto the floor of the empty lounge at Urquhart House.

She ran to the front door and watched while one of the passengers paid the fare. Was Jock there? She looked for a flash of white hair.

They emerged from the cab, the tall one with the beard first, then the smaller one with the leather jacket. He slammed the taxi door and it drove off. Her heart sank.

"Where's Jock?" she called out from the steps.

They glanced at each other as they approached, something wasn't right here.

"Where is he? What's happened? Is he okay?"

Ian climbed the steps first, "Can we come in?"

Rosie sniffled into a tissue, her eyes red with tears. "Why didn't you bring him back sooner? He needed his tablets! You bloody idiots!"

They were sitting in the lounge, around a low coffee table

containing three cups of freshly made tea. Euan glanced at the cover of a Reader's Digest. Full of nice, sentimental articles. The kind of thing old people liked to read, detached from the harsh realities of everyday life. Not Jock though, he lived his life, right to the end. Not a wasted moment. He felt guilt wash over him again for the years he'd wasted with Vicki. No more, he thought. Never again. He took a sip of tea and sat back in the armchair, glancing again at Rosie. She looked familiar somehow.

"He just wanted one for the road," Ian said. "I was going to bring him back after that, honestly. We had no idea. If you'd seen some of the stuff he did tonight you'd never have thought he needed medication. Look, I feel as bad as you, believe me. I feel like I've known him for years..."

Euan said, "He's right Rosie, he appeared fine to us. Didn't mention medication once. He was having a good time. He had some stories eh?..." he looked at Ian, who nodded in agreement.

"I was all over town today trying to find him to give him his bloody tablets too," Rosie stared at the window - their reflections in the glass, lit up by the bright ceiling light. Euan was still puzzling over this girl. He'd seen her before somewhere, he was sure of it. Despite his level of inebriation, which he was starting to feel again, he was beginning to think she was possibly the most beautiful woman he'd ever seen.

"I think we've met before," he said, taking another sip of his tea.

"I think we bumped into each other," said Rosie.

Euan laughed, spitting tea as he remembered, "The Esplanade! Aye, you nearly sent me flying!"

"Yes, I was erm... just in a hurry to find Jock, that's all." She put her hand to her mouth and giggled then sat back and sighed, a long drawn out sigh. "You know his time here was up? He'd only paid until the end of the month. The boss was going to start chasing him for money."

"He didn't mention that," said Ian, "but he did ask me to get a box, said there's a couple of things in there, something for you."

Rosie sat up. "Yes, he's got a box in his room. It's locked though. Come on, I'll show you."

Rosie led them down the corridor towards room 51. "This is it," she said, pushing the door open.

Inside it was just as she'd left it - she'd already replaced the photo of Jock and Ellie on the chest of drawers. Euan picked this up and studied the smiling couple - captured in that happy moment some sixteen years earlier.

"This must be Ellie," he said.

Ian looked, "Christ, they looked so happy. She must have been stunning in her day."

"They were, and I'm sure she was," said Rosie. "Right, the box is in here."

She knelt beside the bed and opened the cabinet, Euan trying not to glance at the curve of her waist as she did so, but failing.

As the door opened Rosie straightened instantly. "Oh," she gasped, "it's not here!"

She turned and looked around the room. She'd definitely put it back in the cabinet hadn't she?

"What did it look like?" asked Ian.

"Big, too big to misplace, took up the whole shelf in the cabinet."

They hurriedly searched the room. Nothing under the bed, on the window ledge, in the wardrobe or in the chest of drawers. There was nowhere else to hide it.

"Shit!" said Rosie, holding her head. "I put it back in there before I left, I swear I did."

"I don't doubt that," said Euan, trying to sound re-assuring. "Could one of the residents have taken it? I mean, they're not all the full-shilling are they?"

"Maybe," said Rosie, "but I can't start waking them up now. I'll ask Sheila, she's been on all night."

They found Sheila in the staff room, brewing her ninth coffee of the evening.

"Hiya," she said, looking Ian and Euan up and down. "Who's your friends? What's up Rosie?"

"Jock's dead Sheila," Rosie said, her voice cracking. "This is Ian and Euan, they were with him tonight."

Sheila hugged Rosie. "Don't blame yourself love, you did what you could." Then turning to Ian, "And what happened to him exactly?"

Ian explained the situation the best he could while Sheila's coffee got cold. Rosie took her mug and poured it down the sink, clicking the kettle on to make a fresh cup.

"Jock asked Ian to get some things out of his box, but it's not in his room. Any idea where it could be?" said Rosie.

"That old box? I don't know. Can't see any of the residents taking it. If they did we'll find it tomorrow."

"Was anyone else in his room tonight?" asked Rosie.

"No," said Sheila. "Well, Fraser was in there briefly before he left for the night, but I expect he was just checking to see if Jock had wandered back in. I was just going into Maureen's room, at the end of the corridor when I saw him. Must have been about eight-ish - a late night for him mind you, he's usually on the golf course by five."

"Did you see him coming out again? Was he in there long?" asked Rosie.

"No, I'd just started sorting Maureen's sheets when I heard Jock's door closing and Fraser heading back up the corridor. Nobody else in here can walk that fast. He was only in there a minute."

"That's all he needed," said Rosie, "the thieving old bastard!"

Their cab pulled up outside a large sandstone villa on Cluny Gardens, a stretch of grand homes in Morningside that reeked of old money.

"Holy crap, he lives here?" asked Ian.

"Yup," said Rosie, "had us all around for a staff Christmas dinner one year - only because he was too tight to pay for a bloody restaurant though. Can you wait here driver please?"

Just then, a small blue van pulled up in front of them. The driver jumped out, stretched, and reached back in for a small toolbox. A bit late for a workman, Rosie thought.

Rosie stepped from the cab and met the man at Fraser's gate. She glanced quickly at the side of the van which displayed a clip-art workman and the words 'AAA Locksmiths'.

"Are you heading in here," asked Rosie.

"Aye, do you live here?" he asked.

"Yes," said Rosie, "although I've forgotten my key. It's okay though, there's someone in." She nodded towards the lights in the living room.

"Okay," the man said, gesturing for Rosie to go first.

Ian and Euan followed up the path, which divided two lawns, as perfectly manicured as the ones at Urquhart House, with shaped conifers lining the route towards the grand entrance.

Rosie rang the bell and smiled at the man. "He'll just be a minute."

She heard footsteps walking down the large hall. She remembered the hall was about the same size as her entire flat, covered with antique rugs and dripping with gilded picture frames.

The door opened. "About bloody time too, I called you hours ago -"

"Hello Fraser," said Rosie.

Fraser stood, like a rabbit caught in headlights. All eyes fell on the old oak box he held at his chest.

Rosie placed her hands on the box, and quietly said, "Now, I don't think this belongs to you Mr Urquhart does it?"

Fraser looked at the box, "I... I was just... you know he'll be thrown out next month don't you? I was only checking to see if he had any more bloody money. I'd have smashed the thing open but it's an antique -"

"He's dead Mr Urquhart," said Rosie, calm now. "He died because you didn't let me phone the police. He died because you failed him. He died of a massive bloody heart attack because you wouldn't let me get his medication to him. Now, unless you want me to get the police involved, I suggest you hand the box over and we'll say no more about it. Your reputation will be intact, and let's face it, that's all you're bloody bothered about."

Fraser let the box go.

"And you'll have my resignation first thing on Monday," added Rosie as she turned to leave.

She strode down the path with purpose, and grinned at Euan as she passed.

The only sound was the diesel rumble of the cab's engine as Ian and Euan turned and followed her back down the path.

"Back to Urquhart House please," said Rosie to the driver.

As the driver pulled a u-turn Euan laughed and said, "Wow, you're a pretty cool customer Rosie."

"I'm shaking like a bloody leaf," she said.

The orange streetlights flashed across the box as they sped back to Marchmont.

"So, wonder what's in it?" asked Ian.

"We'll find out soon enough," said Rosie.

"Shouldn't we have got the locksmith to open it first?" asked Euan.

They paused for a moment as the realisation hit them.

"Me and my bloody Hollywood endings," laughed Rosie.

Back in the lounge at Urquhart House they sat the box on the coffee table, moving their cups from earlier.

"So, don't suppose Jock told you the combination for this?"

"Yes, he said it was twenty, 2 – 0, but it's got four numbers."

Rosie looked at the padlock again. "I've tried loads of things. He used to sing a song while he was opening it, something about a birthday. 'This is the year I was born' or 'this was the year of my birth' - there's a date on the bottom, but it's not that. And I've tried every variation of his birthday. Not sure how 2-0 fits into that?"

Ian thought for a moment, then held the padlock and dialled in 2-0-1-4. The padlock snapped open.

Rosie's eyes met his. "But that's.... now?"

"The year of the referendum. The year of Scotland's rebirth," Ian said.

He unhooked the padlock and carefully opened the box.

Inside was an envelope. Must be the paperwork Jock had mentioned, Ian thought. On top of this nestled a diamond ring, he took it carefully out and held it up to the light. It shone bright and untarnished in the warm glow from the reading lamp. The refracted light danced over her face and Euan's heart skipped a beat. "Ellie's ring; this is for you." He placed it in Rosie's palm.

She stared at it, sparkling in her palm, catching the light just like Jock's eyes used to do, and started crying.

Euan reached into his pockets for a tissue, but only found an old piece of kitchen roll that'd been in there for months. Damn it, he thought, where's the perfectly ironed cloth handkerchief when you need it? He placed a hand on Rosie's shoulder but said nothing. She reached up and placed her palm on his hand.

Ian removed the envelope, crisp, white and fresh. This wasn't an antique - some memory from Jock's past - it was his postal ballot paper for next week's referendum. 'You'll know what to do with that', Jock had said. He checked the ballot paper, it hadn't been filled in.

Pulling a pen from his pocket he read the paper's single

question:

'Should Scotland be an independent country?'

He marked an X against "YES" and placed it in the envelope. One vote, but it could make all the difference. Someone like Jock's vote should count for ten, a hundred even, he thought. His wisdom was worth more than some arsehole voting no based on their football team's colours, or some biased news report they'd seen on the telly.

"Okay, we're done here I think," he said, placing his pen back in his pocket and sealing the envelope. "I'm sorry Rosie, I'll deal with arranging the funeral if you want?"

"No, I'll do it," said Euan, "leave it to me." He pulled Jock's medal from his pocket again, cradling it in his palm, "...it's the least I can do."

"I'll help you," said Rosie, looking up at Euan. She was beginning to think she'd bumped into him for a reason. Okay, he didn't look the outdoor type but he was warm, and funny, and he seemed to like her.

"Well, we'll all do it," Ian said, "I'll pick you up tomorrow Euan, we've got that business at Hunter Square remember? And we'll give you a call in the afternoon Rosie, okay?"

She nodded, scribbling her number on a piece of paper torn from the Reader's Digest. She handed this to Euan, holding his eyes for a heartbeat before asking, "Wasn't there anything for you Ian?"

Ian remembered. "Oh aye, the box. He said I could use it to put my new baby in." He picked up the box, puzzled, it was only about a foot on each side, and about six inches high. Old tarnished oak with black iron reinforced corners and hasp. It would look good on their bookshelf at home he thought. Shona loved stuff like this. She'd probably fill it with pot pourri or something.

"It's lovely, maybe he meant you could use it for the baby's things? First lock of hair, tooth, that sort of thing?"

"Maybe," said Ian, shrugging and placing the box back on the table.

"Okay guys, it's been quite a night, but I think I need my bed. I'll call you a taxi," said Rosie.

Ian stood at the window and watched as Euan and Rosie laughed in the lounge. That awkward laughter that sometimes follows a tragedy. Rosie was gathering up the mugs of tea when the taxi pulled up at the gates.

"That's our cab Euan," he said.

"Okay, right Rosie," Euan said, standing up. "Lovely to meet you. And, like, well done, you know, getting the box back and everything. That was great to watch. And I'll see you tomorrow."

"Nice to meet you too Euan, sorry we couldn't have met in happier circumstances."

Ian grabbed Euan round the shoulder as they walked down the path to the waiting cab.

"Glad to see you happy mate."

"Steady on Ian, early days eh?" He looked at his friend, this big, freckled, ginger tramp of a man and thought, Christ if he can make someone as lovely as Shona love him, there's still hope. Thoughts of Vicki were as far from his mind as they could be. He'd buried her memory already. It was time to move on, the future was bright, the future was... what? Tartan? He thought of Jock, reaching into those red tartan trousers to pull out that medal. Was he thinking what he thought he was thinking?

"So have I managed to convert you?" Ian asked as he opened the taxi door for Euan.

"Let's just say I'm swithering," said Euan. "I don't know, I feel kind of, unshackled. It's weird. I'm not used to positivity."

Yes! Thought Ian, his beard contorted as a smile spread all over his face.

"Where to lads?"

"Royal Terrace then onto Union Street please," said Ian.

"You really need to get a new address," said Euan.

CHAPTER FIFTEEN

Epilogue

John Macpherson's Segway scooter struggled up the slope into his cul-de-sac in Edinburgh's leafy Willowbrae. A cluster of bungalows snuggled into the foothills of Arthur's Seat. The last of the snow had melted, and spring was in the air at last.

He could really do with moving somewhere more accessible, he thought, his old knees were long past walking up this hill. And getting to the castle every day wasn't getting any easier.

He was happy here though, and had lived here for over thirty years. And the neighbours were good - that was important for an old man. You needed decent people next door, and this new family were wonderful. They'd often help him up the hill with his shopping, or call in on him to see if he needed a paper or milk.

He'd been worried at first. Word had got around that it was a young family who'd bought the house - they'd apparently come into money quickly. Not lottery winners he'd hoped, please don't let the peace be shattered by some fortunate louts who'd be having wild parties and parking their bloody motors in front of his drive.

He needn't have worried. The day they moved in there was a lot of curtain-twitching going on in the cul-de-sac, his own included, and he'd recognised them straight away. It was that red-haired family he'd seen in the papers. The father could have done with a shave, but he'd seemed decent enough in the interview. He'd apparently come into the possession of a box made by Deacon Brodie no less, Edinburgh's famous cabinet-maker-turned-thief. It had been left to him by an old friend. Well, it raised a fortune at auction, and here they were. The newest residents of their little leafy enclave. Thank goodness they weren't lottery winners!

It had been quite a time for it, he recalled. Not long before he'd seen them in the papers an ex-soldier, down on his luck, had shown up at the castle one day with a first edition of Adam Smith's The Wealth of Nations. He'd taken the lad under his wing - it appeared they had shared a mutual friend - and arranged for the book to go to auction, and what had it gone for? About £50,000 he recalled. Fantastic stuff, couldn't have happened to a nicer lad. It disgusted him how soldiers who'd served their country could be thrown on the scrapheap like that. He'd bought himself a wee flat somewhere, and a proper lead for his dog.

As he hopped off his Segway he heard laughter from next door's garden, and the sound of their children playing. Oh what he'd give for an ounce of their energy, he thought as he dragged his scooter up the front path.

"Cheers mate," Euan clinked his bottle against Ian's. "She's a wee cracker."

Ian smiled, "Thanks Euan, she is. And as suspected, she's as ginger as fuck." He looked down at his new daughter, just weeks old but already showing a healthy carrot-top.

"Well, you're a family of Fanta-pants; you'd be worried if she was blonde!"

"True," Ian laughed. "So, what about yourself, any plans?" He nodded towards the garden, where Shona and Rosie were sitting at the picnic bench, laughing over a bottle of wine.

"Early days son, early days. Maybe though, you never know..." He gazed out of the window at Rosie, her hair shining in the sun and his heart swelled with love. It did this every time he set eyes on her, and each time he was reminded of Jock's words: Learn from your mistakes, and listen to your heart. He smiled at the memory of their night with that old man. The night that had changed all their lives, immeasurably.

He looked back at Ian, both their noses twitching. "Has she...."

"Shat? Probably." He held Ellie up, the nappy weighed heavily in her white baby-grow. He carefully sniffed her backside, "Oof!" he recoiled, "Come on Ellie, let's get you changed."

Ian laid Ellie carefully on her changing table in the conservatory. "Right, you dirty wee midden, what's going on down here eh?" He made a goofy face and her eyes sparkled back at him.

Fresh nappy on, he lifted her up and looked through the full-length glass windows of the conservatory. The rooftops of Willowbrae and Leith descended towards the Forth - the estuary sparkling in the sunlight as it made its way towards the North Sea. He held her up and said, "Look Ellie, can you see the water?"

Euan appeared at his side. "Cracking view you've got here."

"It's not bad is it?" he smiled. There was a shriek of laughter as Amy and Rory appeared from the bottom of the garden, blasting each other with water pistols. They chased each other around the plum tree. He'd have to find out how to look after that, he thought. When did he prune it? Should he thin the branches out a bit? There was a lot to be learned.

He rested Ellie's head on his shoulder and gently rocked her up and down.

"Did you see that email from Stuart?" Euan asked.

"I did aye, not sure we'll make it over though. Are you and Rosie going?"

"Haven't mentioned it to her yet, but hopefully. Says he's got plenty room for us all."

"He's done a great job on the place. We'll make it over one of these days..."

"The auld alliance?"

Ian nodded. He was looking again at the plum tree. Small green buds had appeared on the branches. He was sure they hadn't been there yesterday. It looked like the long Scottish winter was coming to an end and spring had arrived at last.